CW01628044

Christmas Roses and..

More Stories from Broome Park Prefab Village

(A Fabrian Book)

Pat Posner

Cover Illustration: David Young – http://www.davidyoungillustration.co.uk

Typesetting and Design Fabrian Books – fabrianbooks.com.

Welcome back to Broome Park Prefab Village for this new collection of stories set in the 1950s and celebrate Christmas and other events with the prefab families.

Rationing has ended and there are new products arriving in the shops – though when the weather is cruel, the villagers still have to find ways of 'making do'.

There's love and romance for the young and not so young, worries of keeping secrets, problems and mysteries and the odd crime or two but, above all, friendship and neighbourliness.

About the Author

Pat started out writing children's fiction published by Bloomsbury, Hodder, Egmont and Scholastic.

Nowadays she writes contemporary romance and stories of family, friendship and love set in the 1950s published by DC Thomson, Ulverscroft and Fabrian Books.

Pat lives in a farmhouse on a sheep farm with her husband. They are owned by Tim and Ted, their 2 Rough Collies, visiting wildlife and the sheep who graze in the moorland meadows outside Pat's study window.

For Loretta and Henry – thanks for the walks and talks

Christmas Roses

"There, Audrey. That's the button sewn back on your blouse."

"Thanks, Mum." Audrey walked across to the fireside chair where her mother was sitting with her plastered leg resting on a footstool. "It came off when I was ironing it yesterday. I should have sewn it back on then but I didn't think I'd be needing this blouse 'til tomorrow."

"It's the least I could do seeing as you got a stain on the one you're wearing through helping me *go crackers*."

Audrey's mum had been taken on as an outworker for *Chapman's Christmas Crackers* soon after they'd moved to Broome Park Prefab Village four months ago. Their prefab often smelt of glue and glitter and boxes of finished crackers waiting to be collected lined the hallway. The crackers were collected once a week and all the bits for making more were left in their place.

It could be quite monotonous rolling the crepe paper, gluing it, tying the first end, inserting the little gifts and the rolled up paper hats, tying the other end and then sticking a paper motif, or sprinkling glitter on to each one. The pay wasn't that good but it meant they'd been able to buy distemper to decorate the kitchen and bedrooms and could afford paraffin for the paraffin heaters they needed to use in the bedrooms during cold weather. And in a couple of weeks, they'd be using some of the hard-earned cash for something special.

"I couldn't let you do it all on your own when I had time to do some before I go to work," Audrey said. "Especially as you've taken on more than usual and Dad's working overtime at the brewery."

"It'll all be worth it, though, Audrey. With the extra I earn we'll be able to have a right good Christmas party to thank the villagers for all their help with shopping and bringing round casseroles ready to pop in the oven since I broke my leg. I might even be able to buy you a couple of new blouses so there'd always be a spare ready if one gets stained." Audrey's mum smiled.

They'd been making red crackers today. The crepe paper always stained their hands and, although she thought she'd been careful, Audrey had managed to get a red mark on her white blouse which was part of her usherette uniform. She knew she should have worn something else until it was time to get ready to go to work. But they'd run out of paraffin last night and were waiting for a delivery so her bedroom was freezing.

"I thought wearing my work blouse straight away would mean spending less time in my bedroom when I changed into the rest of my uniform," Audrey told her mum. "By now, it's probably even colder in there, but I daren't chance keeping this on. Gwen would be sure to notice the little red blob when she puts the usherettes on parade."

"She'll notice if you're late, too. You'd best go and put your uniform on and get going. I'll manage to hobble to the door when someone from Chapman's comes. I hope it's Lenny. He won't expect me to help him. He'll do it all himself and I'll make sure he has a drink of dandelion and burdock. He likes it even in cold weather."

Audrey glanced at the clock. "I'm all right for another half-hour yet." She hoped it would be Lenny coming from Chapman's, too. He usually came around this time and if she went to get changed now she might miss seeing him. She had made a few friends since they'd come to live here, Gloria Turner from the prefab opposite and Janet Whittaker who lived in one of the Blakeley Road prefabs. There didn't seem to be any lads her age in the village, though, and working at the Gaumont meant she didn't have much chance to go dancing of an evening where she might have met someone who'd become a boyfriend. But maybe Lenny might ask her out…

A couple of weeks ago when he'd arrived she'd been walking up the garden path carrying a pot of hyacinths. Betty Jones from one of the prefabs on Blakeley Road had given them to her. "Came into flower early this year," she'd said. "I thought they might cheer up your mum seeing how she's laid up with her broken ankle."

Lenny had smiled and said the hyacinths were the same lovely blue as her eyes.

Lenny's eyes were blue, too, and Audrey loved how they crinkled at the edges when he smiled. His hair was a sort of dark caramel. Like the colour of the dandelion and burdock he liked so much.

Audrey remembered how she'd wondered if she should tell him that - but it wasn't exactly a romantic-sounding comparison, so she hadn't.

Last week when he'd called Lenny had admired the white flowers with pink tipped petals growing in a small flower bed beneath the living room window, saying he liked seeing Christmas roses in bloom. She'd agreed, adding they were her favourite flower. At the time she'd thought the few words they exchanged often seemed to be about flowers.

But now, a warm glow flowed through her as she remembered how, looking at her and not the flowers, he'd added: "Pretty as a picture".

Checking the time again Audrey decided to go and change now and take the chance Lenny wouldn't arrive just yet. If he didn't, she'd leave as soon as she was ready and maybe she'd see him going in or coming out of Mary Green's prefab on Blakeley Road. Mary was also one of Chapman's Crackers outdoor workers. She rolled the hats that went inside the crackers. In spring and summer she'd fill an old baby pram with sacks full of hats and push the pram to and from the factory, returning with more to be rolled. You got paid a bit more if you delivered and collected yourself but Mary settled for less in winter and let Chapman's do the delivering and collecting.

Leaving early was a good idea, Audrey thought, hurrying into her bedroom. Lenny might talk more freely when her mum wasn't around. Luckily, she'd put on what little make-up she used earlier. She just had to change into her uniform - a maroon skirt, double-breasted jacket and the white blouse. That done, with cold fingers, she forced her hair into the pageboy hairstyle that looked neat for work, sprayed on some hair lacquer and then dabbed a couple of drops of *Coty L'Aimant* behind her ears.

"You look smart and smell nice, too," said her mum when Audrey went back into the living room.

"I suppose it's not too bad as uniforms go," Audrey said. Then, after checking her mum had everything she needed, she went into the hall. Stretching up over the piled-up boxes of crackers, she grabbed her grey duffle coat from its hook, put it on, raked in the pockets for her gloves and hurried out.

Even though it was fast turning dark, and starting to snow as well, when she turned out of Knott Lane onto Blakeley Road she could make out a lorry parked a distance ahead. She didn't want to miss seeing Lenny come out of Mary's so she walked quickly until she got closer and then slowed down.

But to Audrey's disappointment the young man who came out of the gate carrying sacks piled up in his arms wasn't Lenny. Maybe Lenny was ill. Or he could have had an accident. Or perhaps he'd changed to a different delivery round. She had to know.

"He's taken the day off," the delivery man replied when Audrey asked where Lenny was. "Special event," he added. "Wedding Anniversary."

Stunned, Audrey felt a twinge of hurt deep inside. But she pulled herself together and murmured, "Oh, that's all right then."

It wasn't all right, though was it? she thought as she continued on her way. Lenny had flirted with her and being a married man he shouldn't have done that. Or maybe he hadn't been flirting. Perhaps he'd really been talking about the Christmas roses when he'd said "pretty as a picture". She'd just thought he was referring to her because she'd wanted him to be.

The emotions waged inside her. Disappointment and annoyance that she'd read anything into Lenny's words and the way he smiled at her must have added wings to her feet. When the Gaumont came into sight there was still a good few minutes until her shift started. She decided to go for a coffee and try to calm herself down.

*

As she stood at the counter, someone put a coin in the jukebox. When the record started to play, to Audrey's dismay, it was Frankie Laine and Jo Stafford singing *Christmas Roses*.

And to make matters worse, the girl who served her the coffee said, "I love this song. There's a lovely legend about Christmas roses. It tells of a young shepherdess on her way to see the baby who'd been born in a manger. She noticed the Wise Men and the shepherds carrying gifts and began to cry because she had no gift to give. An angel appeared and brushed over the ground where the shepherdess's tears had fallen..."

The girl paused and smiling said, "This is the part I like the best: And a cluster of white winter roses with pink tipped petals appeared. The shepherdess gathered them to give to the baby. From that time on, winter roses became known as Christmas roses and stand for hope and love and all that's wonderful about the season."

Audrey blinked back her tears as she paid for her drink and went to sit down at a table. Lenny liked flowers. Maybe he knew that legend. Maybe he'd sent his wife Christmas roses for their flaming wedding anniversary, along with his *ever lovin' heart* like it said in the song's chorus. Three times over.

"You feeling homesick again?"

The question broke into Audrey's thoughts and she nodded as a girl with a glass of milk shake sat down opposite her. Like her, Mary was an usherette at the picture house a few doors down. When they'd moved, Audrey had felt really homesick for a while and Mary, who'd also moved away from her old home, had felt the same. They'd often talked about it and tried to cheer each other up.

"I thought I'd got over it," Audrey said now. "But then something happens and it all comes flooding back."

"What do you miss the most?"

"The hills. Being lulled to sleep by the sound of water burbling over a rocky beck, drystone walls, stone bridges, the farm cottage being all on its own with no neighbours except the sheep and cows."

"Sounds boring to me." Mary shuddered. "Might be all right at haymaking time, though, snuggling in a haystack with a brawny young farmer. You've not mentioned one of them, Audrey. Is there a nice farmer you miss as well?"

"There was one or two I went to dances with, but nobody special."

"I don't know why you didn't stop there when your parents moved."

"That's the irony of it. I could have stayed, but I thought it would be nice not living all crushed up with my grandparents and aunt and uncle and cousin. We went to live there after we were bombed out. Mum and Dad wanted to come back to somewhere near Manchester but it took ten years 'til the council offered the prefab. Anyway, when I knew we were moving, I thought I'd happen meet a nice lad who wasn't a farm worker or a blacksmith."

"Maybe you haven't lived here long enough yet to appreciate what there is round here, Audrey. But I suppose, even if you do meet someone, working the late shift at the Gaumont won't do much to help things along."

"Working the late shift doesn't give you much chance to meet anyone in the first place," said Audrey. "I only get to see delivery men and they're either too old, too young or married." An image of Lenny danced behind her eyelids and she sighed.

"You could always go back to Foxleigh, couldn't you?"

"I think I would if Mum hadn't gone and broken her leg so badly. And I probably will once she's had the plaster off. The neighbours have been great popping in and out but Mum still needs someone with her as much as possible until Dad gets home. Otherwise, she'd try to do too much. At least she can do the crackers sitting down. And me working the evening shift means I can help her with them."

"And talking of which," said Mary, pointing to her watch. "It's almost quarter to six."

"Crikey. Gwen will go barmy if we're late for the parade."

Audrey jumped up and rammed on her maroon pill box hat. It was the very devil getting it to stay put on her fine hair. She had to wear it, though. It was part of her uniform.

*

"Are you listening, Audrey?" Gwen asked.

The inspection of uniforms was over and now Gwen was telling the usherettes who would be doing what.

"I'm sorry, Gwen, I wasn't concentrating."

"Our Audrey's feeling a bit homesick," said Mary.

"Or maybe she's lovesick," said one of the other usherettes. "Good job *The Titfield Thunderbolt* is a comedy and not a romance or a weepy."

None of them saw much of the film during the first part of their shift. Their time was spent mainly at the entrance to the stalls and circle. They only went inside to show people to their seats or to check there weren't any trouble makers.

They got to see a fair amount of the feature film during the last showing when it wasn't so busy and they were allowed to go and sit in the seats especially provided for them.

Apart from getting to watch the film, and whisper quietly amongst themselves, it was a chance to rest their aching feet. But Audrey knew if it *had* been a romance or a sad film, she'd have had to think up an excuse for not joining the others.

"Right. If you've quite finished discussing Audrey's lack of concentration, it's time to get your torches and take your places," Gwen said.

But as Audrey walked past, Gwen gave her arm a sympathetic squeeze.

Somehow that small gesture made Audrey feel a bit better. *Gwen's nice really*, she thought, picking up a torch and making her way to the foyer.

*

"We've got a lot in for the last showing, haven't we?" Mary said to Audrey a couple of hours later as they stood by the entrance to the stalls. "Surprising really, everyone coming in says it's snowing hard now."

"Maybe everybody needed cheering up. Seeing a funny—" Audrey broke off as a small group of people walked into the foyer brushing snow off their coats. Amongst them was Lenny with an attractive dark-haired girl clinging to his arm and laughing.

Obviously, they'd chosen to come to the pictures to celebrate their wedding anniversary.

And, Audrey realised after a few seconds, *she'd* have to check their tickets because Mary had gone inside - probably to check everything was all right.

Now Lenny was walking towards her, leaving his wife a few steps behind talking to the other four in the group.

"I didn't know you worked here, Audrey," Lenny said, smiling.

Audrey's heart somersaulted. He looked so gorgeous when he smiled like that. But he'd no right smiling at her as if she were special.

He indicated the people behind him. "It's my parents' twenty-fifth. They always insist on me, my sister and my brother and his wife bringing them here on their wedding anniversary because this is where they first met."

So it wasn't his wedding anniversary. And it didn't seem as if was married after all.

"That's really nice," Audrey managed.

"Not so nice in this weather. How about I walk you home when you finish your shift? If it turns to a blizzard you might get lost. We could get to know each other better, too."

Joy bubbled through her. "I'd like that, Lenny," she said. "I'll sneak my torch out with me so we can see where we're going."

*

They talked a lot on their way to the prefab village. Lenny had told her not to use her torch, adding that they'd hold hands so they wouldn't lose each other in the swirling snowflakes. Audrey thought it was a lovely reason for walking hand in hand. Who knew walking in an almost blizzard could feel romantic?

When they stopped outside the front door of number four Knott Lane, Lenny asked if he could take her out on her next evening off.

"That's about ten days off," she said, sighing. "And it's when—"

"I'll be coming to fetch and deliver the crackers before that," Lenny said. "Maybe we could go for a short walk in Broome Park? The boss wouldn't mind me taking a bit of a break in between deliveries. It won't be so bad having to wait for your evening off then."

"But that's when..." Audrey took a deep breath. "Mum and Dad are having a Christmas party that night and I'll have to be there to help. You could come to it, though, Lenny. If you'd like to," she added, crossing the fingers of the hand Lenny wasn't holding.

"So we'll have a walk in the park and a party to look forward to," Lenny replied. "Give me your torch, Audrey. I want to look at something."

Wondering why he wanted it, Audrey did as he asked and Lenny switched it on and walked a few steps to his right towards the living room window.

He crouched down and swept some snow aside with his hand. "Here they are," he said, playing the beam on the white flowers.

"Someone told me Christmas roses stand for all that's wonderful about the season," Audrey said, wondering why Lenny was looking at them again.

Lenny nodded and returned to her side. "That's probably right. But," he added in a whisper, "I didn't mean them when I said as pretty as a picture last week. It was *you* I meant, Audrey." Then he gave her back the torch, brushed his lips across her cheek and said goodnight.

As she went indoors, running her finger over the cheek Lenny had kissed, she thought of what else the girl in the milk bar said the Christmas rose stood for. "Hope and Love," she murmured before she began to hum the catchy chorus of the *Christmas Roses* song.

Mistletoe Magic

"Shall I carry the bag for you, Grandad?" asked Norman running up to the mobile grocery van where Sam Noble stood talking to his friend and next door neighbour, Amos.

"For crying out loud, Norman. I've only got a little cut on my finger. That doesn't stop me carrying a bit of shopping a few steps across the road to our prefab."

"It's half an inch long and quite deep. That's what Mum said."

"Your mum exaggerates," Sam growled. "It's just a tiny pinprick from the holly I was cutting for the Christmas decorations she's making. I'm surprised she asked me to do it in the first place. There isn't much she lets me help with."

"That's not right, Grandad. She asked you to come and buy stuff from the van."

Sam snorted. "Only because all she needed was a couple of tins of peaches and a tin of cream. And I can get these three things back to her on my own, Norman, thanks very much. So you run off and play with your friends."

Norman sighed before wandering away - his head down and his shoulders hunched.

"You've upset the lad, Sam," said Amos. "He was only trying to help and it's good when a youngster is willing to lend a hand to us older ones."

"What about when us older ones want to lend a hand to the younger ones, Amos? Shouldn't that be a good thing an' all?"

Sam didn't wait for an answer but stomped his way across Blakeley Road. He was right sorry about speaking so harshly to their Norman. He'd have to think of something to make it up to the lad.

It was Ellen making him feel so out of sorts. He just wanted to be useful and do things for his daughter-in-law, especially as she was so busy getting ready for Christmas. But maybe he was under her feet too much.

That hadn't happened when he'd been helping out down at the forge most days. He wasn't needed there now the blacksmith's son was trained up. There wasn't enough work for three of them.

Sam sighed. He missed his little part-time job, the smell of the place and the companionship, the chatter and joking, missed watching the horses being shod – talking to them and stroking them to keep them calm. It had all left a huge gap in his life and he'd no idea how he could fill it.

He didn't know many folk in the village, he'd only come to live with his son and family three months back. He'd known Amos for a long time, though; they'd worked at the same firm when they were young.

"Ah, well," he muttered as he went into the prefab, "at least I've got dominoes at The Woodman this evening. That's if my grouchiness hasn't put Amos off having a game with me."

*

"What's up, Grandad?" Janet asked Amos as she walked into the Whittakers' kitchen where he, her mother and sisters were eating breakfast. "You look right miserable. Did you lose at dominoes last night?"

"He's worried about Sam," her mother told her.

"Right." Janet nodded. "Sam Noble's turned into a real grouch. He wasn't like that when he first moved into number twelve."

"Felicity's worried about him as well," said Vivian. "Says she wants her grandad back how he used to be. She was nearly crying yesterday when she told me how he'd upset Norman."

"Sam feels like he's neither use nor ornament to anyone," said Amos. "He thought since he wasn't needed any more at the forge he'd be able to help Ellen round the place. But she seems to have it in her head that Sam deserves to take it easy now and hardly lets him lift a finger."

"Maybe someone needs to make him feel useful?" suggested Janet.

"Good idea, that is, Janet," said Amos. "But who and how?"

"Is he any good at cobbling? Only my work shoes could do with heeling."

"Likely he is, Janet. He's right good at woodwork and repairing things."

"I wonder if he could fix new wheels on that push-along horse that was Vivian's when she was little?" said Arlene. "You wouldn't mind our Christine having it, would you, love?"

"It's a he and he's called Dobbin," Vivian replied. "And Christine would love him. If fixing him would cheer Felicity's grandad up, that would cheer her and Norman up as well. I don't like my best friends feeling sad."

"What d'you think, Dad? It, sorry, *he* would make a lovely Christmas present for Christine," Arlene said, smiling down at the toddler.

"It's worth a try," Amos said, glad the rest of his family wanted to help Sam.

"Sam will be going to the Community Centre's Christmas Fayre this afternoon with you, won't he, Dad? If I see him there I'll ask him about putting new wheels on old Dobbin."

"And I'll go round after work tomorrow and ask if he can do anything with my shoes," said Janet, as she put on her coat. "I'll be late home tonight, Mum. Daniel's taking me to see *The Ladykillers*."

"Tell that boyfriend of yours he owes me a game of chess," said Amos.

"It's a shame Christmas is only three-and-half weeks off, else I'd ask Sam to carve a chess set." Janet sighed. "I'd love to give Daniel one for Christmas but I can't afford to buy one."

*

"'Afternoon, Pearl," said Amos as their neighbour from number eight came through her garden gate.

"Going to the Community Centre, are you?" Pearl asked.

"Yes. I'm calling in for Sam first." Amos lowered his voice. "He's feeling a bit like he's good for nothing right now. Ellen's a good lass but she doesn't understand Sam needs to be doing things, wants to be useful."

"I were up at Broome Hall this morning doing a bit of cleaning," said Pearl. "And I got chatting to the fella who looks after the grounds and the stables. He was grumbling he was that busy he'd no time to take the horses to be shod. I'll be there again tomorrow. I could suggest he asks Sam to do it."

"That would be grand, Pearl. Right up Sam's street."

Pearl smiled. "He's always been a nice old codger 'til recently. It'd be nice to get him back to how he used to be."

"Not so much of the *old,* Pearl. He's younger than me and I don't feel I'm old yet."

"Same as my mam and Auntie Flo," said Pearl. "They don't feel or act old, either. Tell you what, they're coming to the Christmas Fayre with me. We'll look out for you and Sam and I'll get Aunt Flo to flutter her eyelashes at him. That'll make him feel good."

A warm glow filled Amos as he walked up the path to call for his friend. You could always trust folk in the prefab village to rally round when someone needed help of some kind.

*

Pearl kept her word and Amos hid a chuckle when Flo Harper wandered over to him and Sam and *simpered* at Sam after greeting them.

Amos was trying to edge away when Flo said, "I thought there'd have been some good old-fashioned tree decorations for sale but all I can see are shiny baubles. Connie and I had some lovely wooden figures we used to hang on our tree but we've never been able to find them since we moved here."

What a bit of luck, Amos thought. And completely unplanned as well. "I reckon Sam could help you out there, Flo," he said. "Isn't that right, Sam?"

"I suppose I could carve you some, Flo, as long as you don't want them too fancy," said Sam. He'd not sounded over-enthusiastic but Amos noticed how his friend's eyes had lit up.

There was another stroke of unplanned luck later on when Amos spotted a wooden chess set for sale. The pieces were a bit rough and the black knight was headless but…

"Just look at this, Sam. Our Janet was saying this morning how she'd love to buy Daniel a chess set but couldn't afford one. This is only a shilling and it'd look as good as new if you could do a bit of fettling on it."

"I'll have a go, Amos, but I'll have to make Flo's tree decorations first. And Pearl told me a few minutes ago that the groomsman at Broome Hall might need someone to take the horses to be shod so I'll be going up there to offer my services."

*

"I really thought Sam was back to his usual cheerier self," Amos said to Arlene a week later. "But he was more down in the dumps than ever last night when we went to The Woodman."

"Ellen called round yesterday," Arlene told him. "She said exactly the same. Reckons it's because he's finished all the bits and pieces he was doing for folk. She's right worried about him. She keeps trying to find bits of jobs for him to do around the place. Trouble is, with Christmas only just over a week off, they've put up the decorations and dressed the tree and written the cards. Mostly what's left is the baking and that's down to her."

"When I stopped going out to work I found it hard getting used to just doing bits of jobs instead of a real, proper one," said Amos. "But now, well, I've got used to taking things a bit easier. Especially in winter. Come summer, there's the gardening and such like and other bits and bobs that need doing outside."

"Heaven help Ellen if she has to wait until summer for Sam to feel better. Here, that's our Janet walking up the path. What's she doing coming home from work at this time of the morning? They won't have given her time off, not at their busiest time of the year. I hope she's not poorly."

"We've got trouble at the store," Janet said dashing into the kitchen.

"Not shop-lifting like in that Norman Wisdom film?" said Arlene.

"Even if it is, it wouldn't bring her home, Arlene," Amos pointed out.

"It's the store's Santa," Janet said impatiently. "He's been taken ill. Quite bad he is, we had to send for an ambulance. The grotto's due to open at two o'clock and there's nobody on the staff who could take his place. There's not that many males work there and those who do are too young. So I thought of someone who could do it and went to tell the store manager and he sent me home to ask... See, I thought..." She looked at Amos.

"Oh, no. I don't reckon I—"

"I don't mean you, Grandad. You're lovely and all that but you're as thin as string. We'd need loads and loads of padding to make you look anything like. I was thinking of Sam. He's nearer the right shape and—"

"You're right, lass. Sam would make a good Santa. And being wanted to help out in an emergency is just what he needs. I'll go and fetch him."

*

"If you like being Santa and if the store manager thinks you're good at it, he'll want you for the whole week, Sam," Janet said when Amos returned with his friend. "Just afternoons, so you'd have your mornings free."

"Got nothing else on, lass. I've finished that toy horse for the little'un, done up that chess set for your chap and I took the last of Flo's tree decorations round to her a couple of days ago."

Sam bit back a sigh. He missed walking round to Broome Avenue with a decoration for Flo - who seemed more delighted with every one he made. Put his heart into those wooden figures and shapes, he had. And, if he said it himself, they looked right good on the Christmas tree standing in the prefab's living room window.

Yes, it had been good to have an excuse to see Flo, to choose together which branch to put a decoration on. Sometimes he'd done a little job that needed doing like fixing a dripping tap and putting a new hinge on a cupboard door and, afterwards, he'd sat and chatted for a while to Flo and her sister. Not that Connie stayed with them for long. She always seemed to be "just popping out for a while".

"Our Janet hasn't got all day, you know," said Amos, interrupting Sam's thoughts.

Reluctantly, Sam let go the image of himself and Flo sitting all cosy in front of the fire and tried to imagine himself dressed as Santa sitting in the grotto with an excited kiddie on his lap. That thought cheered him up a little.

"Right," he said. "Ho, ho, ho. Come on, Janet. Let's go."

*

"Does Santa Sam know you're taking our Christine to the store to see him, Dad?" Arlene asked him three days later.

"He does. I reckon he'll be surprised to see Flo Harper with me, though. I think she's really taken a shine to Sam you know. Oh, she was egged on a bit by Connie to start with. But when I told Flo I was taking Christine to Santa Sam's grotto she said straight off she'd ask if she could borrow young Jilly Smith from next door to her and bring her to see Santa, too."

Ellen, who'd called round just as Arlene was getting Christine ready for her outing, laughed. "I reckon Dad will be quite chuffed to see Flo. Those decorations he carved for her, well he took them round one or two at a time instead of waiting 'til he'd finished the whole lot. That had to be because he likes her more than a little."

"Could be," Amos agreed, strapping Christine into her pushchair. "Right, we'll be off. I'm meeting Flo and Jilly at the end of Broome Avenue."

"Before you go, Amos," said Ellen. "The reason I came round was to ask you all to a party on Friday evening. I thought it was such a lovely idea of Beatrice's, her who makes Christmas crackers, to have one to thank the neighbours for their help when she broke her ankle, that we'd have a thank you party, too. Ours will be a couple of days after hers and it's to show how much Keith and I, and the youngsters of course, appreciate the way everyone's tried to buck Dad up."

"That's a lovely idea, Ellen. I'll make you one of my special fruit punches for the kiddies if you like."

"I was hoping you'd say that, Amos. And perhaps you'll pass on an invite to Flo and Connie for me, save me calling round there. Dad doesn't know about it yet, but I'll need to tell him because we thought he might like being Santa at the party, too."

*

Sam gave one "Ho" too many when Amos carried Christine into the grotto with Flo and Jilly following behind. He wondered what Flo would think seeing him fatter and rounder than usual and with a white beard and whiskers, too.

Probably not much. His Santa image was a far cry from Flo's all-time favourite film star Rudolph Valentino – she'd mentioned that she loved him in *The Sheik*. And, Sam recalled, Flo had also told him how she'd cried when he died.

But now, Christine was clambering onto his knee. She chuckled and pulled at his long beard when he asked her what she wanted for Christmas.

"Tell him you'd like a dolly, Christine," said Jilly. "That's what I'd like you to bring me please, Santa. A dolly."

"I'll see what I can do," Sam replied, using his gruff Santa voice. "But for now..." He dipped into the sack with *Girls* written on... "Here's a special early Christmas present from me. And one for the little monkey who pulled my beard as well."

"Thank you, Santa," breathed Jilly. "And it's your turn now, Auntie Flo. You tell Santa what you'd like for Christmas. She isn't really my auntie, Santa," she added, turning back to look at Sam. "I just call her that because she lives next door and she's nice."

Maybe all isn't lost, Sam thought, as Flo came forward, her eyes sparkling and a smile on her lips.

"What would you like Santa to bring you, Auntie Flo?" asked Sam. He winked at Jilly. "I'll call her that because I think she's nice, too."

"I'd like Santa to bring me lots of invitations for outings and for the weekly tea dances at our Community Centre," said Flo. Could you manage that, please, Santa?"

"I reckon maybe I could."

Amos smiled as he caught Sam's eye. "I'd like a stick of some kind to prod a friend of mine when he gets a bit miserable," he said.

"I'll see what I can do. But I've a feeling you won't be needing a stick. I'm hoping your friend will be dancing his cares away."

*

On the evening before Christmas Eve, the Nobles' prefab was bursting at the seams. Sam looked the part, dressed in his Santa outfit. Friends and neighbours chatted away while they helped themselves to some of the delicious snacks Ellen had made and the younger ones ran around with balloons and paper party whistles.

Amos nudged Arlene and, chuckling, pointed to Flo and Sam.

"I told you what Flo said to Santa in the grotto, didn't I? They've spent the whole evening talking to each other. Probably planning where to go on those outings she told him she wanted."

"I best go and tell my father-in-law he'll have to stop his canoodling for now," Ellen said from behind Amos. "No good him dressing up as Santa if he doesn't hand out the presents."

A few minutes later, Sam walked round giving everyone a small parcel from out of his sack. But he left Flo until the last.

"I've a special present for this lady," he said gruffly. "I hope she'll accept it."

"I accept it, Santa Sam," Flo said, blushing as she took her present from him.

"Ah, mistletoe magic," Amos murmured to Arlene when Flo held her present from Santa above her head.

And Sam's grandchildren blew on their party whistles while Amos cheered loudly as his friend drew Flo close to honour the mistletoe tradition.

An Unforgettable Christmas

"Now you won't forget to go straight round to Auntie Betty's after school, will you?" Joy said to Doris and Donald, opening the front door. "And mind you behave yourselves."

"We'll behave, Mum," Doris said. "I hope Uncle Tom will be there, too. But, anyway, it will be like a party. It's a market day today so Dilly, Dinah and Linda Butterworth will be there because Auntie Betty has them until their mum finishes working at her market stall. It's a shame Linda's name doesn't start with D as well, then we'd be able to call ourselves The Five Ds."

"If we come and fetch Pebbles," Donald said, bending to stroke their tortoiseshell cat as it walked down the garden path with them, "we could be the *Five Find-Outers* but it would have to be and cat instead of and dog. The Butterworths love Enid Blyton's mystery books as much as we do so they'd like us calling ourselves that."

"If I find out you got into any mischief like those children in the book do, you'll be in trouble," Joy told them. "But if you're good you can choose the bottles of drink from the *Corona* man when he comes tomorrow," she added as they opened the gate and went on their way down Blakeley Road.

Joy was sure they would behave themselves, they adored Betty and Tom Jones. They weren't any relation, but most of the youngsters in the prefab village called their parents' friends Auntie or Uncle. And Betty and Tom had been right good friends over the years – especially, Joy thought sadly, when my Albert died of influenza. That was coming up to five years ago now and she still missed him something rotten.

Heavens, but it was icy cold out here. "If I don't go back inside, I'll be getting bronchitis or something," she said to Pebbles. "And it's too cold for you to stay out." But she waited until Donald and Doris turned to wave before picking up Pebbles and hurrying back up the path and into the comparatively warm prefab.

Leastways, the kitchen was comparatively warm, though nobody could say the same about the bedrooms, she thought as, after tidying the kitchen and living room, she went to make Doris and Donald's beds before going to make her own. Her bed made, and room tidied, she opened her wardrobe door, wondering what to wear for going to visit her friend in hospital.

There wasn't that much to choose from, but she'd need to dress warm for the journey; first she had to go and draw her Family Allowance at the Post Office, then it would be two bus rides and a train and then a fair walk to the hospital. It might be warm inside though, best to wear the tweed skirt she'd bought on

Radlington market off Maisie Butterworth's *Good as New* rail and a jumper and cardigan under her winter coat then she could take off both coat and cardigan if need be.

Joy went back into the kitchen with her clothes over her arm. She decided she'd close the curtains, light the gas oven, leave the door open and get changed in front of it. And a few minutes later she was stripped to her undies when there was a tap at the back door and someone walked in.

"Blimey, Betty, it's a good thing it's you and not the bread man delivering my two loaves," Joy said, laughing. "I completely forgot to lock the door."

Betty was laughing, too. "Tom offered to bring these," she said, putting a couple of magazines down on the table. "He reckoned I might keep you talking and make you late."

"I always get ready too early when I'm going somewhere," Joy said, stepping into her skirt before pulling her jumper over her head. "We've time for a cuppa before I need to go. I just wish that, if Rosemary had to be taken ill, it hadn't happened when she was visiting her sister-in-law in York I hope I can find my way to the hospital all right, we lived about a mile away from it when I was young. We moved when I was twelve though, so I'm not that sure I remember the area and it will have changed by now anyway."

After turning off the oven and then filling the kettle and lighting the gas under it, she glanced across at the table. "Thanks for the magazines, Betty."

"*Woman's Own* is this week's but *Home Chat* is from two or three weeks back," Betty said. "I remember Rosemary saying one time she was here, she enjoys flicking through magazines. I thought you could take them to the hospital for her, but have a read of them first while you're on the bus or train."

"Rosemary really likes magazines and books with home-making hints and ideas," Joy said. "I always get her the *News of the World Household Guide and Almanac* for Christmas so this *Home Chat* will be right up her street. Oh, I do hope they'll let her out in time for Christmas. She's meant to be coming here you know, and I've been making bits and pieces for ages ready for her visit. Donald and Doris have been looking forward to her coming. They enjoy going to Rochdale for Christmas at hers, but I think they like being here best."

"I thinks it's a lovely idea the way you still take it in turns to go to each other's for the festive season," Betty said. "You've probably plenty of happy memories to share of the times you all spent together."

"Yes. It seemed more important than ever to keep doing it after we were both widowed within months of each other."

Betty nodded. "It was a sad year for you, love."

"I had good friends like you and Tom to help me through," Joy said. "And you've come to the rescue again having my two after school so I can go and see Rosemary."

"If you don't get going now, Tom will gloat because I will have made you late," Betty said, laughing. "And Doris and Donald will end up sleeping at mine, too, because you won't be able to get home tonight."

*

Joy had never been too keen on travelling but, really, she supposed, getting here hadn't been that bad – even though it seemed a long, long time since she'd started out. Rosemary's sister-in-law had said which ward Rosemary was on in the letter she'd sent. Now, Joy thought, as she went inside the building, she just had to find it.

"It's on the third floor," the helpful lady on Reception said when Joy asked the way. "You can use the lift," she added, with a smile. "It's not that long since everyone had to climb the stairs to upper floors but now the lift saves everyone's legs."

Feeling dubious about using it, Joy walked along in the direction of the lift. But, she told herself, it would be something to tell Doris and Donald about when she got home. When she got to the right place, she saw there was a young girl clutching a large notebook and a paper bag, and a lady who was obviously her mother, already waiting for the lift. It arrived all too quickly for Joy and her tummy churned with apprehension as she stepped into it behind them.

"Isn't it exciting?" the girl said. "It would take ages to walk up all the stairs, wouldn't it?" she added, smiling at Joy.

Joy nodded and tried to smile back at the pretty youngster with big brown eyes and sticky-out pigtails.

"We're visiting my gran," the girl continued, dipping into the bag and pulling a yellow sweet and popping it into her mouth. "She's eighty-four and she's going to tell me about Christmases when she was young," she said, in between crunching the sweet. "It's for something our class is doing and I've got to write stuff down and take it to school tomorrow. Mum says I should have done it sooner 'cos now I'll have to rush it."

Her mother nodded and gave a tight smile. Joy noticed she was holding one hand at her throat and her knuckles were white. She guessed her fellow passenger felt even more scared then she did inside this moving cage and tried to think of something reassuring to say. But before anything came to mind, the lift stopped on the second floor.

Joy glanced at the lady who stepped in. She had salt and pepper hair was smartly dressed and had a *Friend of the Hospital* badge pinned on the lapel of her bottle green coat. Then the lift door closed and, as the lift started to move jerkily upwards, two or three yellow sweets fell out of paper bag the little girl was holding.

"Pick them up, Monica," her mum said in a whispery voice.

Monica giggled and, as she bent to pick them up, the lift stopped. "Why's it stopped?" she asked, straightening up without the sweets. "We're not on the next floor already are we? Are we stuck?" she added, her voice rising.

"The lift hasn't been here long, it's still learning how to do things right," said the friend of the hospital, obviously trying to avoid panic.

"I knew we should have walked." Monica's mum gasped loudly. "I hate being in small airless places."

"Mum, I'm s-s-scared," Monica wailed after minutes passed and the lift remained still.

"Not as scared as her mum," the hospital friend whispered to Joy. "I think that paper bag might be needed. I'll get the mum to breathe into it and you try to calm the young'un."

Joy nodded and, controlling her own panic, gently eased the bag from Monica's clenched fingers. She handed it to her companion who emptied the remaining sweets into her coat pocket and then tried to persuade Monica's mum to breathe into the bag.

Joy turned to Monica. "This thing you've got to do for school, Monica. What if I tell you about Christmases when *I* was young?" Joy couldn't tell if her words had registered or not because Monica didn't reply. But she moved closer and snuggled in a bit.

"Well, back then," Joy said, "it always seemed to snow at Christmas. I remember one year near the end of the first world war, when it was hard to find anything very Christmassy in the shops, Mum and Dad crept outside before anyone else was awake and built a huge snowman in the field at the end of our garden. They hid all sorts of tiny hand-made presents in it for me and my sister…"

Joy broke off for a second, and wondered what on earth had made her talk about that particular year when she'd been eleven and her sister twenty-one. It was the last Christmas they'd had together. Almost the last time she'd seen the sister she'd loved so much. It still hurt to think of it even after thirty-seven years.

"What sort of presents?" Monica asked, and Joy came back to here and now. The little girl had sounded calm and the sound of her mum breathing in and out whispered around the lift. They were slow, steady breaths so Joy thought she was calmer, too.

"Well, I remember a tiny rag doll with plaits made out of yellow wool, animals made from acorns, knitted rugs for my dolls' house and… Oh, yes, a wooden flute. My dad made that. He loved music and singing. He wrote a carol one year—"

"Did it get played on the wireless?" Monica asked.

"We didn't have wirelesses back then." Joy shook her head. "No, he wrote it just for us, just for me and my sister. Nobody made a record of it or anything like that, but I reckon it was good enough. Anyway, after I'd tried to play a tune on the wooden flute, Dad took it from me and played the carol and as the rest of us sang it started snowing again. I've always wished someone had been there to take a photograph of us but there weren't that many who had a camera."

"I wish I could have heard you singing the carol," Monica said. "I know what! If you sing it now really, really loudly someone might hear..." her voice wobbled, "...and they'll come and get the lift unstuck."

Joy didn't really want to sing, but she knew she should think of Monica rather than herself so she took a deep breath and start to sing: "Can you hear the Christmas bells? Merrily they're ringing. Can you...?"

She couldn't carry on; the memories were hurting too much. But to her amazement, she heard the next lines.

"Can you hear the Christmas bells? Joyful news they're bringing. Ring-a-ling-ring-a-ling-ring-a-ling..."

"How does *she* know the carol?" Monica demanded. "You said your dad wrote it just for you and your sister. Is she your sister?"

Joy turned round and stared at the woman who'd got in the lift on the second floor and, although she was smiling, there were tears streaming down her plump cheeks. "Hello, Joy," she said softly.

"Belle? Belle, is it really you?" Joy knew it must be and she felt the tears running down her own face. "But what are you doing here?" she asked. "I don't understand."

"She's a friend of the hospital," Monica said. "It says so on her badge. Friends of the hospital come to see people who have no family or friends to visit them. We learned that at school. Now," she added impatiently, unaware of the miracle that had just occurred, "if you carry on with the carol somebody's sure to come and help us."

Joy reached out for Belle's hand and they sang together. "Ring-a-ling-ring-a-ling-ring-a-ling-ring-a-ling, Ring-a-ling-ring-ding-ding."

They sang two more verses, with Monica and her mum joining in the chorus, before the lift suddenly juddered upwards and then stopped on the third floor. The door opened, Monica picked up the sweets that had fallen out of the bag and they all scrambled out laughing and crying.

"Don't disappear again, Belle," Joy begged. "I can't *not* visit Rosemary and you're probably going to see someone who won't have a visitor, otherwise—"

"And we've got to see Gran," Monica interrupted. "Can we all meet up when visiting time is over?"

"I was just going to suggest that," Belle said. "I'll have to get you some sweeties, the ones in my pocket will be sticky and covered in fluff." Then smiling at Joy and squeezing her arm, she added, "My little sister and I have a lot of catching up to do."

*

"We haven't caught up on *all* the lost years yet," Joy told Betty the following morning. It had been late when she'd arrived at Betty's last night but, bursting with happiness she'd told some of the wonderful happening at the hospital before taking Doris and Donald home. And now, Betty had come round to hear the rest of the story.

"I know now," Joy continued as she poured them out a cup of tea, "that soon after our last Christmas together when Belle disappeared out of my life, she'd gone off with someone our parents didn't approve of. She was twenty-one, so pretty and tall and slim, well, she seemed tall to me at the time. She's not slim any more but she hasn't really changed *that* much in looks, not now I know who she is. I think I was so scared of being in that horrible lift, even before it got stuck, that I didn't really take in much about her. Of course I've changed since I was eleven so she didn't recognise me."

Joy took a couple of sips of her tea. "I know I'm rambling a bit, Betty," she said.

"That's not surprising," Betty said. "It's taking me all my time to take it all in, so heaven knows how you're managing to think straight."

"Anyway, Belle didn't need our parents' approval so she got married and then they went to America. Can you imagine going all that way, Betty? It must have taken weeks. But the marriage didn't work out and, after a couple of years, Belle came back to England. She told me she'd been almost broke and too proud to try and find her family. She lived and worked in London but she didn't like it there and a year after the last war ended, she moved back to York, close to where we'd lived as children."

Betty shook her head. "The most amazing thing is that for the last eight years or so, you've been living a couple of hours away from each other without knowing it."

"I know," Joy said. "And if it hadn't been for Rosemary being taken ill while visiting her sister-in-law and me going to see her in hospital on the very day it was Belle's turn of being a hospital friend, we'd never have found each other. Or if the lift hadn't got stuck…"

"But you have found each other and I'm sure you'll be meeting up soon."

"Oh, I haven't told you that bit. Doris and Donald are so excited about this. I never told them about Belle before, because…" Joy had to break off to wipe tears away, "It all happened so many years ago, I didn't know if she was still alive. Now, in less than two weeks, an auntie they didn't know they had will be coming to spend all of Christmas with us. They can't wait to break up from school so they can make special things for her. It's just like something out of one of their story books."

"I love stories with a happy ending," Betty said. "What about Rosemary? Will she be well enough to come?"

"The doctor told her that, as long as her temperature stays down and everything is working normally, she'll be discharged tomorrow. She'll stay at her sister-in-law's a day or two before coming here and Monica and her mum have promised they'll try to visit over Christmas, too. Because that's another *if*, Betty. If Monica hadn't asked me to sing Dad's carol, Belle and I would have parted as two strangers."

*

"Mum, I love how all the stalls have got Christmas decorations hanging up," Doris said. "The ones Donald and I made are nicer though, and there's more of them," she added, as the three of them made their way around Radlington market on the day before Christmas Eve.

"You made so many, I think if we went to all the prefabs in the village and counted up their Christmas decorations, we'd have more than all of them put together," Joy said, laughing.

"And a lot of them are for the tree," Donald said. "I'm glad the ground's too hard for us to dig up the Christmas tree from our garden. It's not big enough to put all of the decorations on. We *can* buy a really big one, can't we, Mum? That's why I've brought my bogey. Even a huge tree will fit on it and we'll be able to pull it along all right with these ropes."

"That's if we can find a big tree," Joy replied. They'd been to three stalls already but the trees were quite small and expensive as well. "I think there's only one more stall selling trees and, even if there is a big one, we won't be able to buy it if it costs too much." She hoped there was only one more stall; it was cold walking round the market even though it was bustling with folk doing last minute shopping. "It's turned even colder since we left home," she added, "so put your balaclava back on, there's a good lad."

"I hope that's because it's getting ready to snow again," Doris said. "Properly this time, not like last week when it snowed hard but then disappeared the next day."

"Not before we get home, Doris," said her brother. "We'd need a sledge to put the tree on then, and this is my bogey. It's got wheels not runners."

"I can see that, silly," Doris said. "And it isn't your bogey, it's ours. Those wheels came off the pram I had when I was a baby."

"No argufying, you two," Joy told them. "Else the bogey will be going home with nothing on."

"It's because we're excited," Doris said. "I don't know why but that does make us argue sometimes. Oh, I can't believe by this time tomorrow our auntie we didn't know we had will be here and so will Auntie Rosemary we've always known but isn't a real auntie and we'll all decorate the tree together. I'm glad we always wait 'til Christmas Eve to do it, then we know the very next morning is Christmas."

Joy laughed, thinking her daughter sounded a bit like the chirruping bird bubble pipes she'd bought to put in the stockings. It was Betty who'd spotted them when they'd gone shopping together a few days ago. And when they'd got home, she and Betty hadn't been able to resist trying them out. She'd only just managed to dry them and hide them away when Doris and Donald arrived home from school. And how the days seemed to have flown since then.

Truth be known, she was probably even more excited than the children about Belle coming tomorrow. She was so looking forward to introducing her sister and Rosemary. She felt sure they'd get on well together. And, like Doris, she hoped it would snow, but not until tomorrow evening.

"Look, Mum, there *is* a big tree here," said Donald, pointing.

"It's seven-and-six, Donald," she said quietly. "I can't afford that much."

She saw Donald's face drop and heard Doris's little sigh. Maybe she could barter a bit, get the price right down.

"It's got good roots so you could plant it out after Christmas," said the stall-holder, coming out from behind his stall where his fruit and vegetables were laid out.

"It's rather straggly," Joy said. "And some of the needles are already dropping off. And it's not worth what you're asking for it," she added, pointing to the price label.

"And Maisie Butterworth who's got a stall over there is a good friend," Doris said, smiling up at the man. "That means you should let us have this straggly tree cheap."

The man roared with laughter. "You've got this young lady well-trained, Missus," he said to Joy. "Give me three-and-a-tanner and it's yours."

"Mum," squeaked Doris as the man helped Donald place the tree lengthways on the bogey and secure it with parcel string, "it's starting to snow."

"Looks like it means it an' all," the stall-holder said. "Safe journey home."

*

"I just hope the guard will let us put it in the guard's van," Joy said half-an-hour later, eyeing the laden bogey worriedly as they stood on the station platform waiting for the train.

"Don't worry, Mum. He will if my clever sister smiles at him," Donald told her.

The guard pretended to grumble a bit, but they all knew he was joking. It was only a short journey, they travelled in the van along with the guard and it wasn't long before he lifted the bogey out and placed it carefully on the platform.

They all thanked him and, after wishing him a Merry Christmas, made their way out of the station. "Now for the walk home," Joy said. It was snowing hard by now, settling on the ground, too. Even when it wasn't snowing, the walk home always seemed longer than the walk to the station.

But they had so much fun on the way back - trying to pull the bogey in a straight line and stopping every now and then to re-balance the tree which kept rolling to one side - it didn't seem long before they were turning onto Blakeley Road. And then they had to keep stopping whenever any of Doris and Donald's friends who were playing out, came over to look at the tree.

"It's got quite a lot of snow on," said one of them. "That's because we've all been singing *Let it Snow* to make it snow harder."

"And *Dreaming of a White Christmas*, as well," added Dilly Butterworth.

"I'm dreaming of getting indoors and having a cup of tea," Joy told them, laughing.

It was well over an hour before Joy's dream became reality. It had been a bit of a struggle to get the tree off the bogey and inside and into the tub they'd left ready to stand it in. But they'd managed it and now Doris and Donald had gone carol singing with the church choir. Joy had promised to join them soon; it would be a lovely ending to a lovely day. And tomorrow would be lovelier still.

*

Belle and Rosemary had arrived within an hour of each other in the afternoon and, as Joy had guessed, they'd got on like a house on fire. Now, Rosemary was snugly tucked up in Doris and Donald's bedroom

- Donald was sleeping on a mattress on the floor so Rosemary could have his bed. He'd told her to hang her stocking up at the end of it and he'd hang his next to Doris's at the end of her bed.

Belle would be sharing Joy's bed just like when they were little. Joy knew Belle wouldn't mind Pebbles curling up with them; they used to have a cat called Timmy who'd slept on their bed. The memories were bitter-sweet, though, Joy thought to herself going back into the living room after she'd whispered goodnight to the children and Rosemary who were all nearly asleep.

"Come on," Belle said, clearly guessing Joy's thoughts. "Stop thinking of what was. Think of what *is,* and help me put these parcels underneath the Christmas tree."

Joy smiled to herself and thought instead of how, back in the old days, Belle always had been a bit bossy - in a nice big sister way.

"I've just peeped outside and I'm sure," Belle continued, "the snow's deep enough for us to build a snowman. I've chosen some of the little presents you were going to put in the stockings in a paper bag. We can still make the stocking nice and bulgy if we fill them up with more nuts, an extra tangerine and one of the gingerbread men Betty made for you. Just think what fun Doris and Donald will have, searching inside the snowman for presents like we used to do."

"I hope the snow doesn't melt away overnight," Joy replied. "I'd like the snowman to last until Boxing Day so we can hide more presents for Monica and her mum. But I want the roads to be clear of snow by then so they can get here all right." Joy touched wood and crossed her fingers.

Belle laughed and did the same. Joy found a torch in case they'd need it and then they both wrapped up in thick coats, hats and gloves, scarves and boots, picked up a bag with tiny gifts in and sneaked out into the prefab's back garden.

It was hard work building the snowman without laughing and talking in case they woke Doris and Donald. Just as the snowman was finished and the presents were buried inside him, the church bells rang out for the Midnight Service.

They both forgot about not wanting to wake the sleeping children as with one accord they began to sing: "Can you hear the Christmas bells? Merrily they're ringing. Can you hear the Christmas bells? Joyful news they're bringing. Ring-a-ling-ring-a-ling-ring-a-ling-ring-a-ling. Ring-a-ling-ring-ding-ding."

Then, arm in arm, they went back inside. "It's going to be an unforgettable Christmas," Joy said. "This time, in the nicest way possible way," she added, hugging Belle.

Snowy Day Birthday Blues

"Quick, Rob. Bring your ruler. These two new ones are the biggest yet."

Jimmy's strident tone woke Pearl from her dream where she'd been somewhere warm and sunny and she sighed as reality burst in. She had a horrible feeling she knew what her youngest was talking about.

Next came Babs' voice - high-pitched and excited. "I'll get you something to stand on, Rob."

A grating noise followed. Pearl guessed Babs was dragging a stool out of the kitchen. Either to the living room or the hall, she thought - knowing she should really get up. That would mean putting on a cheerful act for everyone, though.

She turned her head slowly on the pillow to glance at Alf. He seemed to be still asleep. She didn't have to fix a smile to her face just yet then. Because one thing she didn't feel was cheerful. Oh, not because of the weather - though that didn't help.

It was the fact her birthday was fast approaching and memories of Ruby were crowding in. Her sister was three years older but their birthdays were the same date. They'd made a big thing of it until nineteen-forty-six. In the February that year, a couple of days before their birthday, Ruby had boarded the Queen Mary as a war bride and sailed across the Atlantic to join her husband, Walt.

Oh, she and Ruby wrote of course, but it wasn't the same as seeing each other. Pearl missed her sister something rotten. And it was a good few weeks since there'd been a letter from America.

"The biggest one is five inches long and half an inch round at the thickest bit."

Rob's voice stemmed Pearl's thoughts and then Babs started to sing:

"Over the front door and the window,

That's where the icicles grow, grow, grow

Please let ours the biggest ones be

Then we will win the prize.

Our indoor icicles need to be

Bigger than Bernard's or Graham's you see

Bigger than Ruth's or Vivian's as well

Then we will win the prize."

*

Alf stirred and, grunting, opened his eyes.

"Did you hear what our Babs is singing, Alf?"

"Would've been hard not to. It doesn't sound like it's thawed any overnight, does it? I dunno, Pearl. Only kids could think of having a prize for the biggest indoor icicle."

"I suppose I'd better get up." Pearl groaned as she wriggled round under layers of blankets and Alf's old army greatcoat, trying to get dressed. Keeping their clothes in the bed meant they didn't go stiff with cold - but it wasn't easy to put them on.

"I'm freezing," she added, "and that's before I get out of bed and walk into the hall what sounds like it's full of icicles."

"They always said prefabs were palaces for the people, Pearl. Happen they meant ice palaces." Alf chuckled but Pearl wasn't amused. Thick ice on the inside of the windows, condensation and icicles on the walls weren't her idea of funny.

Before Pearl could tell Alf that, Babs shrieked, "I've made a hole in the ice on the window and guess what, Jimbo? It's snowing really hard out there."

"That'll stop you sounding so airy-fairy about it, Alf." Pearl dug him in the ribs before scrambling out of bed. "The snow will cover all the pathways the council cut yesterday. We're running out of food and we'll never get to the shops with snow on top of ice because the buses won't be running."

*

"Go easy on those *Sugar Puffs*, Jimbo," Pearl ordered. "There's not many left and heaven knows when the mobile grocery van will be able to get here again. Whoever planned the prefab village never gave a thought to bad weather when they built it so far away from any shops. The milkman walked across the top of the hedges to get to us on Thursday. I hope he makes it today, we've only got two pints left."

"And their tops have lifted up with ice," said Rob, walking to the table with a bottle in his hand. "Baggy-me the frozen cream on my hardly here sugar puffs," he added. "Could count them on one hand, I could."

"Don't think you'd even need half a hand to count the spuds or other veg we've got," Pearl said gloomily. "I'm right fed up of this weather now. We've hardly enough food to keep a goldfish alive. Soon, we'll all be like Grandma Grove on that television programme: *Faint from the lack of nourishment.*"

"Why don't you and the other mums do what me and my friends are doing then?" asked Rob. "We've put all our sweets together and we're sharing them out so everyone gets a bit of everything."

"The lad's got a point, Pearl," Alf said. "I bet if you all pooled whatever food you've got left, it would make a jolly good hotpot to share out. We've got that huge saucepan we use for black peas on Halloween and bonfire night. I could turn a dustbin into a brazier and cook over that in the street."

"You two are very good, you know. Very good," said Pearl misquoting the well-known words of the Announcer in the *Goon Show*. "So, right, Rob. If you three and some of your friends go round all the prefabs, tell folk the plan and see if they want to give you some veg or scraps of meat or whatever, I won't mind preparing it all and setting it to cook."

"On my outdoor cooking stove," Alf put in with a grin.

"And," Pearl continued, "if them who can't possibly walk on the snow and ice give you a dish at the start, Rob, you can deliver their hotpot to them. Everyone else can turn up around, say, four o'clock with a dish to get a serving to take home - or to eat on the spot if they want."

"It'll be like a street party." Jimmy leapt up. "Come on, Rob. We'll fetch Bernard and Graham and we can tell them how huge our icicle is as well. Babs can call for Vivian and Ruth and then we can split up to collect food from everyone."

"We'll take the sledges to carry stuff on," said Babs.

"See if anyone's got a couple of bits of coal or coke to spare as well," said Alf. "We'll need fuel for the brazier."

"Nana Connie will have some coke. She had a big delivery not long back." Pearl smiled when she recalled her mother and Aunt Flo moving into a prefab on Broome Avenue just a few weeks before Christmas. They'd both ordered a delivery of coke without telling the other.

"We'll have to go out the back way," said Babs. "We don't want to disturb the icicle over the front door. I bet it *is* the biggest of anybody's. I can't wait to tell Nana Connie about it. It might give her an idea of a decoration for… For something."

The youngsters wrapped up well and hurried off and Pearl felt her sadness creep over her again. She'd guessed the *something* Babs had mentioned was a birthday cake. It'd only be a single layered one. Not like when Ruby had been here and Mam had always made a double layered cake for the shared birthday. Pearl knew her mam would be thinking about their Ruby more than usual as well.

"A hotpot party will be fun, Bead," said Alf. "Cheer us up a bit."

The use of Alf's affectionate nickname for her made Pearl realise he'd guessed she was feeling down and she decided to make a determined effort to count her blessings instead of moping. After all, she should feel glad for Ruby being happily settled with her husband in his homeland.

And Pearl suddenly remembered one blessing. When she'd gone to help Mam and Auntie Flo pack up the old family home ready for their move, she'd found some things she and Ruby had made in the war packed away in the attic and brought them back with her.

"Back in a tick," she told Alf.

She hurried into their bedroom, opened the big fitted cupboard and reached up to pull a siren suit from the shelf.

"Won't look exactly Grace *Kellyish,*" she murmured as she got herself into it. "But give me warm and cosy over glamour any day."

"You look like an oversize pixie," Alf said with a grin when Pearl went back into the kitchen. "Wouldn't mind something like that myself in this weather."

"I know. I should've thought of my old siren suit as soon as the big freeze started. Anyway, love, let's go and get the dustbin sorted ready for you to turn into a brazier because I reckon all the villagers will be taken with the idea and send food back with the young'uns."

*

"Jiminy. Wherever did you get that outfit?" asked Gloria Turner as she walked into Pearl's kitchen. Gloria, with a pair of army socks over her boots and, from the looks of it, wearing two hats under a scarf and at least three coats, gazed in wonder at Pearl's hooded siren suit.

"Cheeky young madam," Pearl replied, laughing. Gloria was half her age but they'd become right good friends since helping P.C. Ken Boyce solve a crime a little while back. "You don't look that great yourself," added Pearl. "As for my outfit, it's a left over from the war when a lot of folk had siren suits like this. They kept us warm in the air raid shelters and this one is keeping me warm now in an iced-up prefab."

"It's a bit grim when we have to wrap up like this for being indoors." Gloria pulled a face. "It's not like we can a get a good fire going in the living room stove. The back boiler might burst if we do. Anyway, Pearl, I came to give you a hand and to tell you Dad's going to attempt walking to Broome Hall across the park and – "

"Surely her Ladyship won't need him in this weather?" interrupted Pearl, recalling Gloria's dad, Bill, was Broome Hall's chauffer.

"No, she'll likely get him to help clear the snow and ice instead of driving her somewhere. More to the point, though, she always has plenty of supplies and Dad reckons she'll give him a few rashers and some kidneys and such-like when he tells her about us lot pooling food to make a hotpot to share round. He thought that a cracker of an idea when Rob and Jimbo told us about it."

Phyllis Clarke said the same thing when she walked into Pearl's kitchen with a few potatoes, a small onion and two sausages a few minutes later. "And I thought I'd come and help with peeling veg, Pearl. I don't know how long it must've taken you to get here from Knott Lane, Gloria. It took me ages from next door but one. I had a right time trying to stay upright."

"You should wear thick socks over your boots," Gloria told her. "That helps a bit."

"It's lucky the young ones don't seem to worry about slipping over," said Phyllis. "I felt green with envy watching them dashing off down Blakeley Road with their sledges."

"I reckon they'll be coming back soon with whatever they've collected," said Pearl. "I'll make us a cuppa while we wait."

"Gosh, yes." Phyllis gasped. "I forget to say your Alf said he was gasping for one, Pearl. He's just lighting that brazier thing. Don't know if you'll be able to use your dustbin for rubbish after, though. He's made a good few holes in it."

"Knowing Alf, he'll find a way of patching it up." Pearl put the kettle to boil and reached for the tea caddy. "It'll be an apology for tea," she said. "I'm running short."

Rob, Jimmy, and Gloria's brother, Bernard, came in through the back door at that moment. Grinning, Rob handed Pearl a packet of tea. "It's from Betty Jones, Mum. She reckoned a few would come round and help and said you'd need it. She sent some turnips and swedes as well and she'll pop round soon."

Bernard and Jimmy put the turnips and swedes and other vegetables they'd collected in the sink. "Almost everybody from this end of Blakeley Road has given something. And there's some oxtail from

Graham Stevenson's mum," said Bernard. "It's already cooked, she was going to make soup with it. Graham's gone off with the girls to collect from the far end of Blakeley Road."

"Has anyone been to Nana Connie's yet, Rob?" Pearl asked.

"Yes, she let us fetch some coke out of the shed. I gave that to Dad on our way in. It were funny though, Mum, when we got to Nana Connie's all the curtains were shut—"

"She probably reckons it'll help keep out the cold a bit," said Pearl.

"And the doors were all locked so we had to knock," Rob continued. "We knocked on the back one first and nothing happened. I was getting right worried. So we hurried round and knocked on the front door. When Nana Connie opened it, she didn't let us in and—"

"We could smell cigarette smoke," said Jimmy. "Like it smells on the upstairs of a bus. So," he added gleefully, "now we know Nana Connie or maybe old Auntie Flo is a secret cigarette smoker. Just wait 'til one of them tells Dad off for having a puff of his pipe and says smoking's not good, that's all."

"That's enough, Jimmy. Any more disrespectful talk and you won't get any hotpot," said Pearl.

"Come on, Jimbo." Rob grabbed his young brother's arm. "You, me and Bernard best go and see if the girls need help pulling the sledges."

Gloria and Phyllis set to sorting and peeling the vegetables while Pearl made the tea. "It's not like Mam or my auntie Flo to be two-faced about anything," she said. "I can't think that either of them was smoking. Mam's always said she couldn't bear the taste or smell. I bet she's got the old paraffin stove going. That pongs a bit and it's likely she didn't invite the lads inside in case they knocked it over."

"That prisoner what escaped a week ago is still on the loose," said Gloria as she scooped out a couple of eyes from a potato. "I remember it said in the newspaper it was thought he might make for Manchester where his family live. We're not that far from Manchester."

"What are you on about, Gloria?" asked Phyllis. "What's that got to do with Mrs Stone and Pearl's aunt smoking or not smoking?"

"You don't think the prisoner might've been hiding out in Broome Park and as the weather got worse and worse he wanted somewhere indoors? I mean Pearl's mum's garden backs right onto Broome Park just like some of the gardens on Knott Lane do. He might have got inside and warned Mrs Stone and Flo not to let on. He could have been smoking when the boys called round and – "

"Honestly, Gloria. You take the biscuit with your imagining, you really do," said Pearl. "I recall Maisie Butterworth telling me a few weeks ago how you once thought someone had a kidnapped girl hidden in the prefab opposite hers and yours."

Gloria grinned. "So I got that wrong. But I've been right about one or two things, remember."

"Yes, you do seem to have a knack for scenting out or getting involved in nasty goings on," Pearl agreed as she poured out the tea. "Right, I'll take Alf's out to him and check if the brazier's hot enough for cooking on yet."

There were two others standing with Alf by his outdoor cooking stove. One was Ken Boyce - the prefab village's policeman and, to Pearl's delight, the other was the milkman with a huge sledge which had milk crates tied onto it.

"You deserve a medal for delivering in this weather," Pearl told him.

The milkman nodded. "When I delivered along Broome Avenue, your mum said the same, Mrs Cole. And you know what? I reckon she's stocking up for a siege. I mean there's only her and her sister but she had six pints off me, plus three bottles of orange juice."

Neither her mam nor her aunt drank orange juice. Pearl searched her mind for a plausible explanation. It couldn't be that Mam was going to put on a party for her on Monday. Mam might be making a birthday cake but she certainly didn't hold with surprise parties.

Filled with unease she looked up at Ken Boyce. "Is that prisoner who escaped a week or so back still on the loose?"

"Why are you asking, Pearl?"

"Mam getting all that extra milk and buying orange juice what she and Auntie Flo never drink and they don't smoke, neither. Yet Jimbo and Rob said they smelled cigarette smoke when they went round earlier."

The police constable looked worried. "I think I'd best go and check on your mother and aunt. I'll call in home first and phone for back-up, but it could take a while for them to get here. Snow drifts have blocked part of the main road."

"You're not waiting for anyone," Alf said. "I'll come with you."

"Me, an' all," said the milkman.

"And I'm not hanging around here when Mam and Auntie Flo might be in danger," said Pearl.

But P.C. Boyce shook his head. "You must stay put, Mrs Cole. But you'll be able to hear my police whistle from here. I promise I'll blow it the second it's safe for you to come round."

"Do as he says, Bead," Alf said, giving her a big hug. "Keep the home fire burning 'til we come home," he added, pointing to the glowing dustbin.

His voice had wavered on the forced joke and Pearl knowing that, really, he was worried out of his mind, nodded unwillingly. "Be careful and stay safe," she whispered.

The three men were almost out of sight when Gloria and Phyllis came out to see what was taking Pearl so long.

"Well, we've put everything we've got so far into the big saucepan along with a couple of Oxo cubes we found in your cupboard," Gloria said after Pearl had told her two friends what was happening. "I'll fetch it out and the hotpot can start getting cooked."

Phyllis nodded. "We can always cook any extra veg the kiddies bring back inside and put them in the big pan afterwards," she said, squeezing Pearl's arm.

Almost as soon as Phyllis had finished speaking, they saw and heard Rob and the six others coming along from the far end of Blakeley Road. "If they keep that noise up I'll never hear the police whistle," said Pearl. "How can I tell them to be quiet without telling them why?"

"I've got some cocoa powder and..." Phyllis pointed to the milkman's sledge. "We've got milk. I'll take them all into mine for a hot drink, Pearl. I'll see to whatever food they've brought as well."

"And I'll take charge of this," said Gloria, arriving with the big saucepan in time to hear Phyllis's words.

Pearl nodded and, in spite of the freezing weather, pulled down the hood of her siren suit. No way was she going to chance missing the signal from P.C. Boyce.

It seemed an awful long time before she heard the welcome sound of the police whistle...

*

"I still can't believe it," said Pearl. "I really can't." Three hours had passed since, skidding and sliding, she'd gone as fast as she could to Broome Avenue.

Now, with portions of hotpot delivered to the villagers who couldn't fetch their own, the others, plus the milkman, were standing around Alf's outdoor cooking stove - eating and chatting happily - while Pearl gazed at her sister and brother-in-law.

They'd arrived in England a couple of days before the big freeze had started, and booked in at a Manchester hotel. Their original plan had been to come to Broome Park village on the morning of the shared birthday. But then with the weather turning and getting worse all the time, they'd set out yesterday morning and, Pearl couldn't imagine how, had managed to get to Broome Avenue last night.

Ruby laughed. "We weren't going to come all the way from America so you and I could be together on our birthday and then not make it in time because of a bit of snow and ice."

"But," Walter said in his attractive drawl, "once we'd got to your Ma's, Ruby was determined you wouldn't find out we were here until Monday."

"And you wouldn't have done, either," said Ruby. "If," she added indignantly, "you hadn't thought that Mam and Auntie Flo were harbouring an escaped prisoner." She giggled and glanced at Walt. "One who smokes *Pall Mall* cigarettes."

"Still, better safe than sorry," said Gloria. "And hearing all the ins and outs has certainly taken everyone's mind off the weather."

"My mind's back on the weather," said Rob. "That is, it's back on other thing what happens when it's freezing cold. We haven't taken anyone to see the icicles over the inside of our front door yet."

"Oh, yes," Babs shrieked. "Can we take Bernard and everyone in and show them, Mum? Then we can claim the prize for having the biggest one."

Pearl smiled and nodded. Having Ruby here made her feel as if she'd got a special prize of her own.

Secrets

Connie Stone poured herself a cup of tea and sat down to read the letter from her best friend back in Liverpool. Always wrote a nice newsy letter, did Mabel.

But this time, Connie realised as she got half-way down the letter, Mabel's news was a problem in the making:

I know your prefab's only got two bedrooms and you and Flo have one each. But I was wondering if you'd fancy a lodger for a couple of months or, happen, more. I'm made up they're going to put a bathroom and inside lavvy in, Connie, they'll be starting on it in about six weeks. I can't stop here while the work's going on and there's no room for me at my son and daughter-in-law's.

You told me the bedrooms are a fair size and it wouldn't be the first time you and me had shared a home and a bedroom, would it?

"That was almost forty years ago, during the First World War," murmured Connie. "And Flo didn't come into the equation then."

And, heck. Here was Flo now. Connie folded the letter and shoved it in her pinafore pocket just as her sister hurried in looking anxious.

"Was that the postman I heard while I was in the bath, Connie?"

"Paper boy delivering the *Saturday Gazette* most likely," said Connie.

She pointed to the unopened newspaper thinking how lucky that it had been delivered almost at the same time as the post. There'd only been the one letter and she didn't want to mention that to Flo yet.

"Oh, right." Flo pursed her lips and nodded.

"You look disappointed, Flo. Are you expecting a letter?"

"No, not really." Flo put her hands around the teapot. "Gone cold. I'll make a fresh one."

Connie watched her walk over to fill the kettle. Flo didn't seem her usual self. Come to think of it she'd been a bit quiet this last week or two.

Sam Noble hadn't been calling round much, either. He and Flo had become friendly last Christmas time and since then they'd been going to tea dances and having days out together. But Sam hadn't been a large part of Flo's chatter recently.

"*An Alligator Named Daisy* is on at the pictures, Flo. Donald Sinden's in it, you like him, don't you? D'you fancy going to see it this evening?"

"Sam and I thought we'd go and see it. Diana Dors is in it, too. Sam, being a fella, likes her. You could come with us, Connie."

"No thank you. Two's company and three's a crowd," said Connie, glad Flo and Sam were obviously still friends.

"Three being a crowd's when the couple's a young courting couple. Not when they're *Twerlies*."

Connie smiled at the Liverpool word for those getting on in years. "Twerlies or not; three's still one too many, Flo."

Actually, Connie was relieved on two more counts. One, she hadn't really wanted to go to the pictures but had thought it would cheer Flo up if she was feeling a bit down. And, secondly, being in on her own would give her a chance to write back to Mabel.

That's if she could come up with a good excuse for not having her friend to stay. She could do with talking it over with someone.

"Don't pour me another cuppa, Flo. I'm going to pop round to see Pearl and the grand-kiddies. I'm longing to hear if Rob's got a place as an apprentice painter and decorator. I can't get over him being old enough to work in a month or so. He's still wet behind the ears, bless him."

*

Connie's probably going to show Pearl that letter I'm sure I saw her slipping into her pinny pocket, Flo mused, watching through the kitchen window as her sister hurried down the path. I wonder why she didn't want me to know about it.

Well, she wasn't the only one keeping secrets, was she! Shrugging, Flo poured a cup of tea and went to sit down.

The secret she was keeping – hers and Sam's – had been hiding in her heart for a while now. She still couldn't believe she'd been so impulsive that day. And as for dear Sam's reaction…

Hugging the memory to her, Flo smiled. Fancy this happening to them at their age. But really it was their age causing a problem. And, although she didn't want to keep things hidden from others, until they could find a way around the problem, the secret had to remain between her and Sam.

Hearing a light tap on the window she looked up. Her heart beat faster when she saw Sam's smiling face; it were as though thinking about him had conjured him up.

"Come in," she called and pointed to the door. Then, telling herself she was acting like a soft young lass, she ran her hands over her hair and jumped up.

"I saw Connie walking past and guessed she was going to Pearl's," he said.

Flo nodded. Pearl's prefab was next-door-but-one to where Sam lived with his son and family.

"So," Sam continued, "I thought it was a good chance for us to be alone together. See, there's summat bothering me, Flo, love."

"Come and sit down and tell me," she said. But a shadow had crossed her heart. Maybe Sam was having second thoughts about…

"It's Keith and Ellen," said Sam, tugging at one ear the way he always did when he was worried.

Briefly, Flo was relieved to hear it was Sam's son and daughter-in-law causing his worry. Then scolding herself for her selfishness she asked, "How do you mean, Sam. Is one of them ill?"

"I don't reckon that's it. But either they act over-bright when they speak to me or they start to say something and then seem to change what they'd been going to say. And I saw Keith signing a bit of paper which he tucked inside his newspaper right quick when he noticed I was in the room."

"You know, Sam, earlier on I saw Connie slip something into her pinny pocket and I had a feeling it was a letter she didn't want me to know about."

Flo thought for a moment. "Do you think we're imagining things because we know we're keeping a secret from them and feel guilty about it?"

"I don't know, love. Could be that I suppose. And if it is, maybe we should come clean and tell them."

"We said we'd wait until we've solved our big problem, Sam. And I don't know if we *can* solve it. Not the way we want to, anyroads."

"Put the kettle on and make us a cuppa, Flo, and we'll have a bit of a think."

Flo did as he suggested though she didn't reckon - how ever much they thought - they'd come up with an answer that wouldn't cause hurt and worry for Connie and Sam's family.

*

"See, Pearl," Connie said to her daughter as they sat in Pearl's living room drinking a cup of tea, "like you know, Mabel's been my best friend since we were Rob's age.

"Been through a lot together, we have. It will really upset her if I don't write back and tell her she'd be more than welcome to stay a while. But…"

"Auntie Flo isn't that keen on Mabel." Pearl nodded. "I remember how she steered clear of her at any parties or outings we had."

"I don't know why," Connie said. "I asked Flo once and she said it wasn't that she really disliked Mabel, she just couldn't take to her so it was best not to spend long in her company."

"So you're faced with either upsetting Mabel if you don't ask her to stay or upsetting Flo if you do."

"Flo has seemed a bit down about something this last couple of weeks as well," said Connie.

"She looked right miserable when I saw her the other day," Rob said. He, and his sister, Babs, had just brought in some biscuits and slices of cake. "She must have been to pay the rent because she was coming out of the Housing Office."

Puzzled, Connie gazed at her grandson. "It couldn't have been Flo. The rent man comes round collecting the rent. And what were you doing in that neck of the woods anyway, Rob?"

"Painting a shop door over the road from the Housing Office place. Well, it was my boss-to-be doing the painting. I was watching to see how it should be done. Learning a bit before I start on as his apprentice. And Dad said I could paint the shed door. I better go and a bit of practise in right now.

"But it was Auntie Flo I saw, Nana Connie," he said as he walked towards the living room door. "She didn't see me, though."

"Well, if it was her, Pearl, she's not told me why she went there," Connie said. Though she felt sure Rob had made a mistake.

"There's a lot of not telling things going on lately," said Babs, munching on a biscuit. "I thought Felicity Noble was my best friend but she can't be because best friends tell each other everything. Felicity's got a big secret and she won't tell me what it is."

"It's likely something to do with your birthday with it being just two weeks off," Connie said.

"Oh, Nana Connie, you're a corker. I never thought of that. I'll go and call for Felicity now and I won't ask what her secret is."

"If only I could solve my problem that easy." Connie sighed as Babs dashed off.

Pearl laughed. "Give us your tea cup, Mam, I'll read the leaves and see if there's any answer on its way."

Pearl swirled the cup three times then upended the cup on its matching saucer to drain away any liquid.

"Right," she said peering at the patterns the tea leaves had made inside the cup. "There's an angel here, see? That means good news. And here's a boat. That means a visit from a friend."

"Very clever, Pearl," said Connie who believed wet tea leaves were for rubbing on work surfaces to remove smells and not for telling the future. "So, happen Mabel's visiting and the good news will be she'll only need to stop for a day or two."

"That will mean domestic changes," said Pearl. "Just like this thimble here is forecasting."

"Right, now the tea leaves have told me Mabel will only be staying a little while, happen I should go home and mention it to Flo." Shaking her head, Connie stood up.

"Oh, ye of little faith," Pearl said, laughing as they walked to the door together.

It would be a weight off my mind if I could have faith in the tea leaves, Connie thought as she walked down the path and opened the gate.

She hadn't gone far when she saw Babs dawdling along, head down.

Oh, dear, had her grand-daughter and Felicity had another falling out?

As Babs drew close, Connie saw the tears rolling down her cheeks - heard the choking sobs.

"Whatever's the matter, Babs? Have you hurt yourself?"

"It's that secret Felicity was keeping, Nana Connie. She…she… the whole family's emigrating to… To Australia. Got a special cheap ticket or something. And I'll never see my best friend again."

"Are you sure, Babs? Maybe Felicity was teasing you or playing make-believe."

"She was *not*. She was crying. And her mum came in just as Felicity were telling me and Felicity is in big trouble because she weren't meant to say anything. I'm going now. I want my mum."

Connie watched until Babs had gone inside and then walked on. She felt right sorry for Babs and Felicity. And no wonder Flo had been quiet and a bit down with Sam going to Australia. Such a shame when the two of them had become such good friends.

As she rounded the corner into Broome Avenue, Connie found herself face to face with Sam.

"Just been to see Flo," said Sam.

"And I've just seen Babs," said Connie. "She told me how you Nobles have become *Ten Pound Poms*. Flo will miss you a lot, Sam. I hope you'll write regular to her."

"What the heck are you on about, Connie?"

"Oh, I know it was meant to be a secret but your Felicity went and let it out to Babs how you're all going to Australia on a cheap ticket."

Sam stared at her and then a strange expression crossed his face.

"Do me a favour, Connie, and don't drop even so much as a hint of this to Flo. Not yet. I'll sort it soon, you have my word."

*

"It's coming up to two o'clock," said Flo. "Let's turn the wireless on, Connie, and listen to *Melody Mixture*."

To be honest, it wasn't one of Flo's favourite programmes but she had to do something to try and stop her sister chattering. Talked non-stop, she had, ever since coming back from Pearl's. Connie often did that if she was worried or nervous about something.

Likely it was to do with the letter I'm sure I saw her hiding, Flo thought.

They'd only just settled down when there was a knock on the back door.

"That's Sam's special knock." Flo jumped up. "He's already been once today and I'm seeing him this evening. I wonder why he's here."

"If you let him in, you might find out, Flo."

"Flo," Sam said when she opened the door, "I want you and Connie to come round to Blakeley Road. Keith and Ellen have got big news and when you've heard what it is..." He leaned forward and gave her a quick kiss, "I reckon we'll be able to tell them our news."

"Right." Puzzled but hopeful, Flo called to Connie to turn the wireless off. "And put your coat on. We're going round to Sam's," she added as she walked off to get her own coat.

*

Sam smiled across at Flo as she listened in astonishment to his son and daughter-in-law breaking the news that they and the children were going to Australia. For good.

"We were that worried about telling Dad," Keith said.

"We knew he wouldn't want to come with us but I couldn't bear the thought of him being on his own," Ellen added. "We just couldn't find the right moment to tell him."

Sam chuckled. "But then I unexpectedly heard about it through a third party so I asked Keith outright if it were true. And of course it is. So, now, Flo, my love, shall we tell them—"

"Sam. Them going off to t'other side of the world doesn't solve our big problem," said Flo.

"Oh, but it does, Flo. See, when I moved in with them last year, Keith added my name to the rent book. There shouldn't be any problem about me taking over tenancy of this prefab. So…"

Joy bubbled through Flo as she realised what that meant.

"You mean I can stop going to the Housing Office and begging them to find us a prefab here because we can live in this one together."

Connie cleared her throat. "Are you really telling us you and Sam want to live together, Flo?"

Sam chuckled again. "She is, Connie. But not 'til after I've made an honest woman of her. Your Flo proposed to me on February 29th. Leap Day. And I accepted with bells on."

"Flo. I didn't know you had it in you to do something like that," Connie said. "Nor to keep it secret from me, neither," she added.

Flo felt herself blushing, but Connie was smiling kindly.

"Sam and I were keeping quiet until we could find somewhere to live," Flo explained. "I was worried about leaving you, Connie. But I knew if we could stay in the village we'd still see each other all the time. Only they didn't hold out much hope at the Housing Office for me and Sam getting allocated a prefab here, but said they'd write and let me know if anything did come up.

"It's our age, see. They said any vacant ones were more likely to go to young marrieds wanting to start a family or them with children already. And Sam—"

"I was worried you'd miss having me round to keep an eye on our Felicity and Norman when you and Ellen were at work, Keith, and doing odd jobs round the place," Sam told his son.

"But now," Ellen said, laughing, "you'll have your own new life to lead. You'll have to get wed before we leave, though."

"Quicker the better for me," said Sam. "When you're lucky enough to find love at our age..."

"We don't want to waste any time we could be together," Flo agreed.

"How long before you go, Ellen?" Connie asked.

"Seven weeks, on the last day of June," she replied.

"Enough time to arrange a lovely wedding, I reckon," Connie said. "And having it before you leave could solve two more problems."

Reaching out to touch Flo's hand, Connie explained about the letter from Mabel.

"I couldn't think of having her to stay before I heard your happy news, Flo, love. But now I won't have to upset either of you."

"We'll invite her to the wedding, Connie, and she can stay as long as you both want," said Flo. She was glad Connie would have her best friend around for a while.

"What's the other problem Flo and me getting married will solve, Connie?" asked Sam.

"Babs and your Felicity being upset about things. How do you fancy having your great-niece and your grand-daughter-to-be as bridesmaids, Flo? Choosing pretty dresses and such-like might help take their minds off Felicity going to Australia a bit."

"I think that's a wonderful idea," said Flo. "Don't you, Sam?"

"I do, my love."

"We can tell all our friends we're getting married when we see them at church tomorrow," said Flo. "Oh, I'm so glad all the secrets are out in the open."

"Me, too," said Ellen. "We'll drink to that. Should be champers really but we'll have to settle for tea."

"Happen we should get Pearl round to read the tea leaves," Connie said. "She read mine earlier and she saw good news and domestic changes."

"Don't need tea leaves to tell us we're going to have a happy life together do we, Flo?" Sam said, smiling lovingly at her.

Wrong Number

"Zip-a-Dee-Doo-Dah." Maddie heaved a sigh of relief as she made a right turn off Blakeley Road onto Broome Avenue. She always felt a bit nervous when driving the *Reliant Regal*. She'd only got a motor cyclist licence which meant the reverse gear on the 3-wheeler had been blanked off. If she'd driven past Broome Avenue, she'd no idea how far she'd have to have gone before she could turn round to get back here. And, now, here was number two where her sister Doreen, brother-in-law, George, and their young daughter lived.

Maddie turned off the ignition and leaned back in her seat. She and Doreen had never got on particularly well. It was more that they tolerated each other because they were sisters; Doreen hadn't asked her to be a bridesmaid when she'd got married and they'd never seen much of each other even before George and Doreen had been allocated a council property and moved to a different area. It had been quite a surprise when she'd got the letter from Doreen asking her to come and stay for a week: *Mum wrote and told me you'd been really poorly with flu and you weren't recovered yet. It's like being in the country here, there's a huge park at the bottom of the garden and the springtime air is so fresh. Do come, Maddie. I've enclosed a little map for you.*

Leaning forward, Maddie glanced in the mirror to check her hair - and pulled a face. She really wasn't sure about her *Poodle Cut* hairstyle. Going from long, straight hair to permed curls might not have been such a good idea. And she was nearly twenty-eight, was the style too young for her? "Too late now to worry," she said aloud. She got out of the car, grabbed her case and then stood and stared.

The prefab didn't look very big from the outside, it couldn't have more than two bedrooms, could it? She shrugged and supposed she'd be sharing her niece's bedroom. Jilly was five and Maddie hadn't had much chance of getting to know her. It would be good to put that right. And maybe absence had made the heart grow fonder and she'd get on better with Doreen.

Well, she'd soon find out, wouldn't she? A flicker of apprehension coursed through her as she opened the gate and walked up the garden path. When she reached the front door, there was an envelope with her name on pinned to it. Maddie just *knew* she wouldn't like the contents. She plonked her case down, tugged the envelope free and ripped it open…

*

The key's next door at number three. Sorry, we won't be here, it's school holidays so we're going to Rhyl for a few days. You can sleep in Jilly's room. Please keep an eye on the council decorators, tell them I want blue paint not green.

After reading the brief note, Maddie was in half a mind to turn round and go home instead of going to the prefab next door to fetch the key. Of course, if she hadn't been suffering from after flu lethargy, she'd have realised there'd been an ulterior motive for the invitation. And Doreen hadn't actually said in her first letter that they'd be here, had she!

Fighting down her irritation, Maddie told herself that spending time on her own might make a pleasant change from working in her parents' hardware shop and she could always go home in a couple of days if she felt like it. So she scrumpled the note and, leaving her case by the front door, she made her way to number three.

"Ah, you must be Doreen's sister come for her key. Maddie, isn't it. Come in. I'm Flo and you'll see my sister Connie in a minute. You'll have to excuse her," she said lowering her voice. "She's got a bit of a cob on because the paper boy delivered someone else's magazine to us again."

Flo looked to be in her seventies and seemed a friendly sort and Maddie couldn't help smiling. "Do you both live here?" she asked.

"We moved here from Liverpool so Connie could be near her daughter and son-in-law and grand-kiddies," Flo explained. "They live on Blakeley Road. Rob, the eldest lad is here now. He's fifteen and starting work in a week or two. Come on through to the living room and meet them."

They'd only taken a couple of steps towards the living room when a boy, Maddie knew must be Rob, came out into the hallway. "I think I've persuaded Nana Connie not to report the paper boy, Auntie Flo. He'd likely get the sack if she did. I think she's madder at me for telling her *Tit-Bits* isn't a rude magazine," he added with a cheeky grin. "There's a picture of Joan Collins on the front and she were in *Our Girl Friday* that Nana Connie took us to see just after you moved here and that wasn't a rude film it were a comedy."

"Thank you for that information, lad," Flo said, clearly trying not to laugh. "This is Maddie. She's Doreen-from- next-door's sister, she's staying there a while."

"Hello, Maddie. Nice to meet you," Rob said politely.

"Sorry, queen, I don't know your surname," Flo said, turning to Maddie.

"It's Wood. But I don't mind if Rob calls me Maddie. Miss Wood makes me feel like...like a school teacher or something." She'd almost said spinster but wasn't sure if Flo had ever married and she might not like the word spinster.

"Right, I'll be off now," Rob said. "I'll pull up some of that chickweed by your front gate on my way out. I promised I'd take our Jimbo to Broome Park. We can feed the chickweed to the rabbits in

Pets' Corner and then he wants to collect frogspawn from the big pond. Tara, Nana Connie," he added, glancing over his shoulder as a lady with a round, plump face appeared in the doorway.

Flo smiled and introduced Maddie to Connie. "We'll put the kettle on in a minute, but first, come and sit down for a bit," Connie said, walking back into the room. "It's good to meet new folk. And you've come to keep an eye on things when they start painting our prefabs, haven't you?"

"Doreen told us they'd be away when they come to paint them so she asked you to come and stay so you can make sure theirs didn't get painted green," Flo said.

Connie nodded. "It's good when you can do things for your family. Though I couldn't help my eldest grandson out today. He wanted one of my old stockings to make a fishing net and I haven't got any I could let him have."

"We sell fishing nets in my parents' hardware shop," Maddie told her. "But if a little one comes for one and hasn't enough money, I suggest them using a fine hair net to make one."

"That I can do, and Rob's probably still picking chickweed," Connie said, as she bustled out, calling to Rob.

Flo laughed. "Dotes on her grand-kiddies, my sister. There's Barbara as well, she's the middle one. She loves your little niece. Calls for her every Sunday to take her to Sunday school."

"That's nice," Maddie said. "It's a shame they're in Rhyl, though. I was looking forward to seeing Jilly."

"Didn't you know they wouldn't be here?" Flo asked.

"I thought I might see them before they went," Maddie replied – not wanting Flo to know how Doreen had omitted to mention anything about them going away. Then, feeling her annoyance creeping back, she added, "I won't stay any longer now, Flo. I want to get unpacked and then have a look around."

Flo got to her feet and walked over to the sideboard. "Here's the key," she said, taking out of a fruit bowl and then handing it to Maddie. "But you must call round for a cuppa and a chat sometime soon."

"I will, and thank you," Maddie said.

She saw Connie and Rob on her way out and Rob gave her a thumbs up. "A hair net was good thinking."

"I hope you get some frogspawn or maybe some sticklebacks," she said before making her way back to her sister's prefab.

*

Maddie scooped up the newspapers from the doormat and wandered into the kitchen. The novelty of having time to read over breakfast, and having nothing she *had* to do afterwards, was starting to wear off. True, she'd enjoyed the first three days wandering around the prefab village in the glorious spring weather. It was so different from the built-up, rather dismal area she lived and worked in. As Doreen had said in her letter, it was like being in the country.

All the prefabs had good-sized gardens and the scent of daffodils, violets, primroses and wallflowers, what Maddie thought of as cottage flowers, filled the air. There was blossom on some of the trees, too, and every time she glanced across to Broome Park, Maddie wished she had a book on trees. In between her exploration, she'd chatted to the painters who'd painted the outside a pretty blue and met some of her sister's neighbours.

Perhaps that's why she was feeling a bit down, though. Two of the neighbours she'd met were around Doreen's age and happily married with young children. Maddie had hoped for that sort of life for herself and Roy until, after finishing his National Service, he'd decided he wanted to emigrate. She hadn't wanted that at all and after one particularly bad row, their relationship had ended. That was over six years ago and she really should have got over it by now.

It was strange really how things had worked out. Doreen, determined to stay single and become a secretary, had got married and left her job as an office typist. And Maddie, whose dream had been to live in a country cottage with honeysuckle and roses around the door and to be a housewife and mum to three children, was still working in her parents' hardware shop.

True, Doreen wasn't exactly living the life Maddie had dreamed of. The prefab was nice and well-planned but it wasn't an old country cottage with two storeys and nooks and crannies and beams and low ceilings. As she stood in Doreen's kitchen, pouring *Quaker's Sugar Puffs* into a bowl she could hear a cuckoo calling and glanced out of the window and across to Broome Park to see if she could spot it. The beauty surrounding her, making her think of what might have been, hurt. Really hurt. But she'd given up her dream of living somewhere like this because Roy had belonged in that dream and without him it was meaningless.

She walked over to the table and put her cereal bowl down with a thump. This is why she wouldn't have come if she'd known she was going to be on her own, being alone gave her too much time to brood. But even though she knew that emigrating, living in a far off, alien country, wouldn't have been for her, she'd never managed to get Roy completely out of her mind. And had never found anyone else she wanted to live her dream with.

Her tummy rumbled reminding her she was hungry. She reached for the milk bottle and poured milk onto her cereal. In spite of her mood, the novelty of having milk ice-cold from the refrigerator hadn't worn off yet. And she might as well read the newspaper seeing as it was here. She unfolded it and tucked inside was a *Jack and Jill* comic.

Her niece probably liked the name so similar to hers, Maddie thought. But as she idly glanced at the front cover, her eyes were drawn to the writing in black pencil at the top right-hand corner: *2 Broome Lane*. So was the comic for Jilly or not, or had the comic been delivered to the wrong address? Though, perhaps the newsagent written Broome Lane when it should have been Broome Avenue? But Maddie recalled how Connie next door had been annoyed about the paper boy delivering someone else's magazine to her and decided to go next door after breakfast and ask if there was a Broome Lane in the village.

*

Rob was at Flo and Connie's when Maddie went round and asked about Broome Lane, explaining why she wanted to know.

"There is a Broome Lane," Rob said. "It's not in the prefab village. It's a row of old cottages behind Broome Hall. It would be quicker for you to drive there but you can walk to it through the park. It's a right nice walk and there's a gate at one side of Broome Hall that leads onto the lane. I could come some of the way with you, I'm meeting some friends at the boating lake."

"I'm not sure Maddie were thinking of taking the comic there herself, lad," Connie said.

"I might as well," Maddie replied. "I expect the little poppet it was meant for will be feeling disappointed."

"D'you know there's a way into the park over a stile?" Rob asked Maddie when they set off a few minutes later. "It's there, see, just next to number four, the Claytons' prefab, where the road curves."

Maddie nodded. "The Claytons keep hens, don't they? I met Mary Clayton and one of her children the other day."

"Yes, Nana Connie gets eggs from them sometimes," said Rob. "But are you all right to climb over the stile?"

"I might seem old to you, Rob, but I'm not too old to do that."

Rob grinned. "Didn't mean it that way. Even Nana Connie climbs over it at times. I thought you might be worried about getting your foot caught in your skirt or something," he said.

"You could have a point there." Maddie glanced down at her polka-dot circle skirt. "I'll just have to be extra careful."

She managed to climb over without doing any damage but thought she might get grass stains on her skirt when they walked through the long grass.

"It's only a small stretch like this," Rob said. "See, there's a proper pathway just ahead."

"I bet you spend most of your time here during the school holidays," Maddie said, looking around once they were on the path.

"Usually at the big pond or the boating lake," he told her. "And I'm going to make the most of this school holiday. It's the last one I'll have. I'll be goin' out to work after Easter."

"Do you row around the boating lake or just watch others?"

"Don't tell Nana Connie," Rob said, "but if me and my friends get there before the fella who sells tickets for the boats, we go for a swim. I'm wearing swimming trunks under my trousers."

"We lived near Rochdale when I was about your age," Maddie said. "A few of us used to cycle to an open-air swimming pool in a moorland village and then spend most of the day swimming."

"Shame you aren't wearing a cozzie under *your* clothes, Maddie. You could have joined us in the boating lake. But here," Rob added, "is where I leave you." He pointed ahead, "Just keep walking that way and you'll see the gate at the side of Broome Hall."

It wasn't too long before Maddie went through the gate onto Broome Lane. Her breath caught in her throat as she gazed at the short row of cottages; her dream had been to live somewhere like this. She made her way around two parked vehicles then slowly walked up number two's garden path noting the riot of forget-me-nots, primroses and narcissi on one side and wild flowers on the other. Thinking it best to hand the comic over in person, she knocked on the front door.

A harassed looking woman who, thought Maddie, was probably around the same age as her, opened the door. Maddie introduced herself, held out the comic and explained how it had been wrongly delivered to her sister's prefab on Broome Avenue.

"Your sister must be Doreen Smith. Her Jilly and my Hazel are great friends, they sit together at Sunday school. You don't fancy coming in and giving the comic to Hazel yourself, do you, Maddie? Though I must warn you, she's got a bit of a cold. She's grumpy with it and when her comic didn't arrive with the newspaper it was a bigger deal than it would usually have been. She's only five and the mood she's in, if *I* explained things, she'd likely blame me for the wrong delivery. I'm Amy, by the way," she added.

Maddie couldn't refuse and, anyway, she was a bit curious to see if the inside of the cottage lived up to her dream cottage, too. Though she knew it would hurt if it did. She followed Amy in and Amy called up the stairs for Hazel to come down. "I'm sorry she feels so out of sorts," said Amy as they walked on into the kitchen. "I think I'd have a bit more patience with her if it had been any other day. But I'm giving a dinner party this evening, my husband's been working away, it's our sixth wedding anniversary soon, so it's a sort of welcome home, anniversary celebration and catching up with friends."

Amy sighed. "I don't think he reckoned on having to do the food shopping for the party by himself. We need quite a lot and it will be easier to stash it in the car boot instead of carrying heavy bags on a bus. I can't drive and I wouldn't want to drive our car anyway, it's too big and I'd be scared. We'd planned for all three of us to go shopping, but I can't face dragging Hazel round the shops the mood she's in."

Amy wound down and shook her head. "What must you be thinking of me? I don't usually babble on like that. I'm just a bit stressed today. Ah," she added, "here's Hazel. "This is Maddie, Hazel, she's staying at your friend Jilly's and she's brought something for you."

Even though she was scowling and had tear-stained cheeks, Maddie thought she was a pretty little thing. "Hi, Hazel," she said. "I've brought your comic, I'm sorry but the paper boy delivered it to my sister's by mistake."

"Have you read it?" Hazel asked.

"Not really," Maddie replied, "I just looked at Jack and Jill and their little puppy on the front cover. I love that little puppy."

"I saw a toy puppy just like Jack and Jill's Patch in the toyshop. Daddy's going to buy it for me so I can play with it when the party's on," Hazel added.

"Daddy mightn't have time to go to the big toy shop in town for Patch today, sweetheart." The deep, male voice had come from behind Maddie and she froze. Surely it couldn't be? But he continued speaking and she knew she wasn't mistaken. It *was* Roy. She knew his voice as well as she knew her own.

"He's got to do all the food shopping on his own because Mummy's staying here to look after you. But maybe I'll manage to find something special to bring back."

Hazel tugged Maddie's hand. "If Mummy goes as well, Daddy will leave her doing the shopping while he goes to go to the big toy shop," she said, gazing earnestly at Maddie. "If you stay and look after me, I'll let you read my comic and we can play with my toy farm. I pretend it's Buttercup Farm where Jack and Jill live."

Stay here where Roy's living my dream with Amy! A dream he said he couldn't share – didn't want – but it's their sixth wedding anniversary so he obviously married Amy and came to live here just three months after we'd split up.

"Please, Maddie. I'll be good, I promise."

Maddie shook her head. She couldn't stay here and look after Roy's daughter. "I'm sorry, Hazel, but—"

"Maddie? Maddie. It can't be." Maddie heard Roy move, knew he was walking round from behind her and swallowed hard.

He's hardly changed, thought Maddie, staring up at him. His hair – how she'd loved running her fingers through it – was still as dark brown, his grey-green eyes still made her feel as if she were melting and his mouth...

"You've changed your hair," he said. "It was long and it never used to be curly. But what on earth are you doing here, Maddie? I knew you'd – "

"Maddie brought my comic," interrupted Hazel, twirling round to face him. "She likes Patch the puppy but she mustn't like me 'cos she won't stay and look after me. If you'd said yes," she went on, turning back to speak to Maddie, "Daddy could've gone and got me Patch while Mummy did the other shopping. And the toy shop might sell out if I don't get one today so if I never get one, it'll be all *your* fault," she ended on a sob.

"Hazel," said Amy, moving to put her hands on her daughter's shoulders, "I know you're upset but that doesn't excuse you being rude to Maddie. I think you better say sorry."

"No, no, it's all right." Maddie managed to look away from Roy. "I've got things to do at my sister's, Amy," she said. "I'm walking back through the park and it's a lovely warm morning. The walk here made me feel better even though I've got a bit of a cold." Even through her distress Maddie managed to word it so that Hazel might not guess that she was offering to look after her at Doreen's. "I know you don't know me, Amy, b-but Roy does. *Did,* I mean. And you do know my sister."

"Are you sure?" Amy asked. "It would be a tremendous help, Maddie."

Maddie nodded. "And don't feel you have to rush, Amy. I'll make some lunch for Hazel."

"Does that mean…are you going to stay and look after me, Maddie?"

"I'm taking you back with me, Hazel," said Maddie. "Jilly's mummy's got a lot of brass and it got dusty when the outside of the prefab was painted. I've got to polish it, you can help me if you like."

"And can we read my comic as well?"

Maddie nodded. "From cover to cover." She glanced at Amy. "Is Hazel allergic to anything?" she asked.

Amy pulled a wry face. "Only to being disappointed. She likes most food, she's not a fussy eater."

"She loves home-made battered fish," Roy put in, staring meaningfully at Maddie.

How could he? How dare he? The two of them used to make that regularly in her parents' kitchen at the house they'd lived in back then. Used to have fun testing if the batter was too thick or too thin. And…

"Can you make battered fish, Maddie? It's my *betsest* favourite food," said Hazel.

"Not one for giving delicate hints." Amy smiled at Maddie.

A pain sliced through Maddie's heart. She hadn't made it since she and Roy split up. And to make it now knowing it was for Roy and Amy's daughter…

But Hazel looked so hopeful. "I bought some fish off the fish van yesterday," Maddie said at last. "I was going to poach it. I'm not sure if there's any plain flour in Doreen's cupboard, though. But I'll make batter if there is, Hazel."

"You sounded all croaky then." Hazel giggled. "Like a frog with a sore throat," she added. "I hope there is some plain flour in Jilly's mummy's cupboard," she added.

Roy moved towards one of the cupboards; Maddie had always loved the way he walked with long, lithe strides. She tried so hard not to watch him but her eyes wouldn't listen to her brain. He opened the cupboard, reached in and picked something off a shelf. Then he turned and walked over to Maddie. "Plain flour," he said, holding the packet towards Maddie.

For one moment, Maddie thought she could see a hint of sadness, or regret, on his face. But she must have imagined it because he looked away from her and, smiling, ruffled Hazel's hair. "Have a lovely lunch and be good for Maddie, sweetheart. I'll see you later."

Hazel smiled up at him. "You'll be bringing something very special, won't you?"

"I will indeed," he said, winking.

Maddie knew she had to get out right now; the pain in her heart had become a sick and fiery gnawing. "If you get Hazel a coat and anything else she might need," she said to Amy, "we'll be on our way."

It seemed to take Amy for ever to fetch a coat, to button Hazel into it and kiss her goodbye. "Mummy or Daddy will come and collect you to bring you home," she said to the little girl. "And thank you so much for doing this, Maddie, you're an angel."

Maddie mumbled a reply then, keeping her head down to avoid making eye contact with Roy, she took Hazel's hand and they hurried away.

*

"There," Hazel said an hour or so later, "the brass is so sparkly I can see my face in everything. 'Specially in the big horse-shoe, I can even see how blue my eyes are." Hazel had chattered non-stop, asking questions and telling Maddie about sitting with Jilly at Sunday school and the things she liked doing, all the time they been polishing the brass.

Maddie smiled. "Now, let's wash our hands and then we'll make your batter."

Hazel giggled. "You mean the fish's batter, Maddie."

Luckily, Hazel kept up her stream of chatter while she watched Maddie cooking and that helped a little to stop too many memories from crowding in. It didn't stop all of them though; the once familiar aroma of fried fish brought tears to Maddie's eyes.

She knew she'd have to eat at least a small portion to keep Hazel company and was amazed that she somehow managed to do so. Hazel said she was too full for any fruit so, after Maddie had cleared away, they went through to the living room to read Hazel's comic.

"I like these lacy things over the back of the armchairs," said Hazel. "They're like the stuff on a princess's wedding dress. Did you have a lacy dress when you got married?"

"I've never been married," Maddie replied.

"Why not?"

Maddie replied without thinking. "I loved someone once—"

"When you do get married, you will have a lacy dress won't you? And as well can I be your bridesmaid 'cos I've never been one?"

It wasn't likely that she'd ever get married but she couldn't say that to Hazel. "Only if you let me be your bridesmaid, too," Maddie replied over the lump in her throat.

They'd just finished reading the comic for the second time when the doorbell rang. "I expect that's your mummy, Hazel," said Maddie. Please, please, please don't let it be Roy fetching Hazel, she prayed as she went to open the door.

Her prayer went unanswered.

"You look a bit up-tight, Maddie," Roy commented as they went through the hall into the living room. "Has she driven you crazy?"

"Not at all, we've had a lovely time," said Maddie.

"I'm going to be Maddie's bridesmaid," shrieked Hazel, "and did you get the very special thing?"

"I did." Roy replied abruptly, then looked hard at Maddie. "How can she be your bridesmaid when you're already married?" he said.

Maddie shook her head. "*I'm* not married, Roy. What gave—?"

"Uncle Roy isn't married, either," interrupted Hazel. "He told Mummy he'd been an idiot, a fool, and he'd lost his only love. He even made something gorgeous for her. It's in his workshop, I've seen it."

"B-but, I d-don't understand," stuttered Maddie. "You're Hazel's dad, it's your sixth wedding anniversary, you…you… When you walked into the kitchen you told Hazel you had to do the shopping on your own - said you might not have time to go and get a Patch toy."

"Hal was upstairs getting ready," Roy said. "I told Hazel that her daddy might not have time to get Patch. I said *I* might manage to find something special to bring back. Are you really not married, Maddie?"

Maddie shook her head.

"I went looking for you a year after we'd parted," Roy continued. "I knew I'd made a terrible mistake months before that but I wanted to do something before coming to find you and that took a bit of time. I went to your parents' house but you'd all moved. The old lady living there said your mum and dad had bought a shop somewhere but she didn't know where and that you'd got married and she didn't know where you lived either."

"That was Doreen, my sister. She and George lived near me and my parents for a while when we moved and then they were allocated this prefab. Are you really not Amy's husband? I still don't understand."

"*Daddy* is Mummy's husband, silly," Hazel said. "Uncle Roy is my daddy's brother. He had to make up a fib to tell Mummy why he couldn't stay and look after me 'cos he was fetching the very special thing." Hazel giggled. "Have you hidden it, Uncle Roy?"

Roy nodded. "In Broome Park's old stable block, sweetheart."

Maddie stumbled to a chair, sank down and covered her face with her hands. "I think my flu's come back," she moaned. "My temperature must be sky high because I can't understand anything."

The next second, she felt Roy pulling her hands gently away from her face. "Can you understand I love you? That I talked a load of rubbish that awful day we split up and I've never stopped regretting it and have never stopped loving you?"

Hazel squealed. "Is Maddie your lost love? Are *you* the one Maddie loved once? I think she still loves you, her eyes are all shiny, I can see from here. Oh, that's million-billion-gold-star-good 'cos I really, really like Maddie. She'll be my auntie when you get married, won't she?"

"Roy, did I hear right?" Amy rushed into the room. "The front door was open so I just walked in," she said. "Did I hear right? Is Maddie…are you getting—"

"Did Daddy get me a Patch puppy, Mummy?" asked Hazel.

"Yes, he did, sweetie. He's waiting outside in the car with it. We didn't know Uncle Roy had come to fetch you until we saw his van outside. Now, hush because I want him to tell me—"

"Buzz off, Amy, and take Hazel with you," said Roy. "Maddie and I have a lot to sort out."

When Amy and Hazel had gone, Roy pulled Maddie to her feet and kissed her. A gentle, fleeting kiss but, thought Maddie, one full of hope and promise. "I want to take you somewhere, Maddie. It won't take long and I'll explain properly on the way. You will come, won't you?"

Maddie nodded.

"Hal's bought Amy a small car because she'd love to learn to drive and she'd be scared to drive his *Singer* because it's quite big," Roy said once they'd set off.

Maddie nodded. "Amy said she couldn't drive. I can, but only a 3-wheeler car on a motor cyclist licence."

"The car's to be a surprise and today seemed a good day for him to give it her," Roy continued. "Anyway, Amy needed a couple of extra chairs for the party tonight, so Hal and I planned that I'd deliver them in my van."

"I saw this van parked near Amy's," Maddie remembered.

"I use it for work. But we told Amy I had a special appointment and didn't want to arrive in my van so I'd go in their car and they'd drop me off on their way to do the shopping. They dropped me round the corner from the car showroom, we let Amy think I was seeing a prospective client."

"And you drove her new car back and it's hidden in the old stable block at Broome Park." Maddie laughed. "I really thought I was delirious when Hazel and you were talking."

"That's nothing to how I felt when I discovered you weren't married," Roy said.

A few minutes later, he pulled up outside a carpentry workshop. "We're on the far end of Broome Lane, the other side of the Broome Hall from Hal and Amy's," he explained. "Back in the day when there was a huge staff at the Hall, this was their resident carpenter's. I remember telling you once I liked working with wood.

"But," he added bitterly, "I never told you that I didn't think it was prestigious enough to do as a full-time thing. I was such a fool, Maddie; Hal has always travelled around for his work, seen different places and foreign countries. I wanted to be one-up on him and go and *live* in Australia or New Zealand. I was determined to do anything Hal did but to do it better. One-sided sibling rivalry," he admitted. "Hal's great and he'd have had a fit if he'd known. Anyway, hop out, Maddie and let me show you round."

Inside, Roy pointed out various items of furniture in different stages of completion. Maddie could see that even the unfinished pieces were going to be exquisite. She ran her fingers over the back of a chair, enjoying the warmth of the wood, enjoying touching something Roy had touched.

"Now for the first piece I ever made," he said. He took her through to another section and pulled a protective cover from…

"It's an old-fashioned love-seat." Maddie gasped. "Is this what Hazel was talking about, Roy? It's beautiful, really beautiful."

"I made it for you, Maddie. That day I went looking for you, I wanted to bring you to the workshop, show you what I was doing here and then take you to the cottage I'd bought. A cottage with honeysuckle and roses around the door. I'd taken the love-seat to the cottage; it fits perfectly in the inglenook in the cottage living room. When I heard you were married, I brought it back here, but I couldn't bear to part with it. I didn't part with the cottage, either, Maddie. Would you like to come and see it? It's next door but one to Amy and Hal's."

There was no mistaking what Roy was really asking her. Maddie could almost feel the shadows that had lived in her heart for so long fading away. But she and Roy would never have found each other again if hadn't been for Doreen looking out for herself as usual. Oh, it didn't bear thinking about.

"Maddie?" Roy asked.

Maddie wound her arms around his neck. "Only if we take the love-seat with us," she said huskily.

Easter Parade

"What's up with you, Bernard? You've got a face on you like when Smokey chewed a wasp."

"You're more like Smokey than I am with your *catty* remarks," Gloria's brother replied.

"I'd rather be a cat than a grouse like you, *bearish* Bernie."

"Honest to goodness, Gloria," said their mum, "you're eighteen and still act like a kid at times. As for you, Bernard, what are you doing sitting indoors on a day like this? I'm sure all your friends are doing something outside."

"They are," Bernard said. "Doing stuff that's for little kids. They're collecting flipping Pussy Willow to wave around on Palm Sunday and after that they're going to use the twigs to decorate prams and bikes and bogeys for the Easter Parade. It was right good when we did Easter stuff up at Broome Hall last year. I wish we were doing it up there again instead of us having to do something here in the village."

"I bet you're glad it's not happening up there, Mum," said Gloria.

"Too true. Organising the Fun Day last Easter nearly finished me off. I wouldn't want to do that again, not for a big clock. And talking of clocks, look at the time. I'll be late for the lunch-time opening at The Woodman if I don't get going. Landlord likes his barmaids to be there early."

When their mum had gone, Bernard carried on where he'd left off. "And seeing how we are doing it, I wish I could think of something good to do, something better than sticking twigs onto flipping toys."

"Egg-rolling would be fun, *ar kid.* Why not do that? Go up to the folly in Broome Park and roll them down that big slope. You'd need to hard boil and decorate the eggs first of course."

"I'd need some eggs in the first place," Bernard snapped, but Gloria could tell he quite liked her idea.

"Tell you what. I've got to go along to Broome Avenue. I've got a Toby Jug for Connie Stone. Spotted it on Duggie and Sid's pot stall when I was at Radlington market yesterday. I could call in on Mary Clayton and see if she's any eggs to spare. Her hens usually lay well this time of year."

"Right. Ta, Gloria. We'll need eggs for something even if we don't have egg-rolling."

*

"I don't reckon Mary's even thought about collecting eggs today," Connie said when, after presenting her with the ornament, Gloria told her about the egg-rolling idea. "Her John was rushed in yesterday morning with appendicitis. He were operated on straight away. Flo and I had the kiddies sleeping here in case she needed to go to the hospital. When she collected them an hour or so back, she said John would be all right but would be off work for quite a bit."

"Where does he work?" Gloria asked.

Connie shrugged. "Funny, but neither of them have ever said and I never liked to ask. Just know he leaves early in the mornings on his *NSU* moped. Maybe he's a tax inspector or something. Some folk might not feel at ease with him if he is."

"Well, whatever he works at, I'll spread the news that he's in hospital and then everyone will rally round to help in some way. Mary will likely get enough casseroles and loaves of home-made bread to feed an army. I'll call in now and see if there's anything she wants doing or fetching. Maisie Butterworth had some men's dressing gowns on her *Good as New* rail yesterday. John might need one if he's to be in hospital a while."

*

"I told Connie I was coming to ask you about eggs for egg-rolling," Gloria said when Mary led her into the kitchen. "Then she said how your John was in hospital. How is he? And if he needs a dressing gown, I could bring you one from Maisie Butterworths' stall tomorrow. She's got some right nice ones."

A dressing gown would be useful, Gloria," Mary said gratefully. "John's has seen much better days. Felt a bit ashamed when I took it in for him, along with his pyjamas and slippers. Not that John would worry about that. What's worrying him, even more than not being able to go tatting for a good few weeks, is Moses."

"Tatting? Is that collecting rags and bones and stuff like a totter does?"

Mary gave a half-smile. "There's a few different names for it, some not very nice, but, yes, John is a rag and bone man."

"And does Moses work for him?"

"Moses is his donkey. John's got a yard and stable in Salford. He says Trevor, the chap in the yard next to his, will feed and water Moses but Moses loves working and gets depressed if he isn't out pulling the cart most days. I feel sorry about Moses of course, but sorrier still that we won't have John's earnings coming in."

"I've often wondered how totters turn what they collect into money," said Gloria.

"John stores all the stuff he's collected in his yard 'til the end of every month and then takes it to the rag yard and the scrap metal place and gets it weighed in for cash. He doesn't often get bones, but if he does he sells them to a place that turns them into fertilizer."

"Cripes, it's not the end of March for another couple of days. Does that mean—" Gloria broke off. It might sound nosy asking if John had taken March's stuff for weighing in.

Mary nodded. "It means no wages this month. I reckon I can just about manage somehow for a few weeks and the stuff will still be there when John can get back to it. But if it takes a while for him to be fit enough…"

"What if someone went tatting for him and just kept adding to the stuff in the yard 'til John can take it for weighing in? Then you'd have a couple o' month's earnings in one hit, even though you'd have had to wait for it."

"That'd be a miracle," Mary said.

"Easter's coming up, and it's the time of year for miracles, isn't it? I think I've got an idea. I bet Moses knows his way round the places John goes, just like the milkman's horse knows which houses to stop at."

"You mean you think you know of someone who might go out collecting with Moses and the cart?"

"Can't promise, but I might," Gloria replied. "I'll bring you a dressing gown for John tomorrow evening and I'll let you know then if I've been successful. And if I have you could ask John about it and, if he's for it, you could write down the names of roads he goes collecting on."

"Either way, I'll make sure I'll have a few eggs for the egg-rolling on Easter Sunday," Mary said.

*

"Don't be a twerp, Gloria." Her dad shook his head when she put her idea to him. "I know you've driven a pony and cart for events her Ladyship puts on and, fair enough, it's good you want to help Mary out. But going round the streets blowing a horn and callin' out for rags and stuff is no job for a lass."

"I've never heard the like," said her mum.

"She'd be good at calling out," Bernard put in. "You're always saying she's got a voice like a foghorn, Mum."

Gloria ignored her mum and brother and concentrated on persuading her dad. "It'd only be two or three times a week for a month or so, Dad, just 'til John's fit again. And I wouldn't be letting Maisie down, I'd still do Wednesday, Friday and Saturday on her market stall and go rag 'n' boning on the other week days."

"That's not the point. John's a big fella and can cope with any aggro he might get in the back streets—"

"He likely goes round the posher areas where the big houses are. And, anyways, I could borrow Laddie from Jenny Pearce. I saw her after I'd left Mary's and she was telling me about him growling and barking at the decorators when they were painting her prefab. Said he sounded right scary even though he's a big softie really. And I've often taken him with me when I've gone on a bike ride, so he'd enjoy walking alongside me when I ride over to John's yard."

"I can see you've thought it all out, Gloria. Tell you what. If her Ladyship won't mind her chauffer driving a donkey and cart, I'll ask for a bit of time off next week and come with you a time or two first to see if I reckon you'd be safe on your own, how would that do? It'd be that or nothing," he added.

"You're on, Dad. Of course, we don't know if John will agree to it. If he does, Mary will get details of where he goes and anything else we'd need to know."

"What I know is that you can twist Dad round your little finger," Bernard said. "It's not fair just because you're a bit older than me."

"When you're old enough to leave school and start work, little brother, happen you'll want to be a totter," Gloria told him. "And Dad would find it hard to say no seeing how he's going to be one for a couple of days."

"That's a couple of days too many if you ask me," Gloria's mum said. She clearly didn't like the idea at all.

*

"So how did it go today?" Gloria's mum asked the following Tuesday. Was it as good as yesterday?"

Gloria nodded, thinking Mum seemed to have come round to accepting things a bit more now. "You'd never believe the stuff we got, Mum. Some of what folk call rags are better than my Sunday best outfit."

"What were they dressed like themselves?"

"Like John told Mary, it isn't often the lady of the house comes out to the cart in the posher areas. They send one of the maids. They were wearing sort of uniforms really. I felt right sorry for them, most wanted a goldfish because they aren't allowed proper pets of their own."

"More than a few wanted a blown-up balloon today, Edith," said Gloria's dad. "Reckon they were the nursery maids wanting a little something to brighten their charges' day. I got fair out of puff at times."

"Should have let me go instead of you, Dad," Bernard grumbled. "Blowing up a few balloons wouldn't get me out of puff."

"But you've been with Gloria twice now. Do you think she'll be safe enough to handle it on her own, Bill?"

Gloria waited anxiously for her dad to answer that question.

"Trevor, the fella who's got the yard next door to John's seems a right good sort and says he'll give Gloria a hand unloading into John's storage room as well as keeping a good eye on Moses. And if Thursday goes like today, I'm sure she'll be all right on her own, Edith. You should hear her yelling *Raaaag-Bone,*" he added with a smile. "Never thought I'd see the day when I were proud of the way she can shout."

"Thanks, I think, Dad," said Gloria. Then she turned to her mum. "We'll be going around streets of terraced houses on Thursday and, according to what John told Mary, most folk there will want a donkey stone for their rags. So we'll take plenty with us."

"That takes me back to when I was a lass in Liverpool. All the housewives there cleaned their front steps and window ledges with donkey stone. I wonder if they're called that because it's often a donkey that pulls a totters' cart."

"I don't know. But Moses is a lovely donkey, Mum. A few kiddies run out to stroke him and talk to him and he laps it up."

"I wouldn't mind seeing to Moses when you get back to John's yard and are busy unloading stuff, Gloria," Bernard told her. "I could ride over about four o'clock or whatever time you finish. I like donkeys and I'd like to do summat useful as well."

Even though he drove her crazy at times, Gloria felt sorry for her younger brother who was at the horrible in between age of too young for some things and not old enough for others. But she did have something in mind and, if Mary thought it would be all right, it would cheer Bernard up no end. She didn't dare even hint at anything, though, 'til she'd spoken to Mary.

"Mum, I'm going round to Broome Avenue now," she said, "to let Mary know how me and Dad went on."

*

"Come in and tell me all about it," Mary said, coming to meet Gloria as she walked up the garden path to the prefab. "The children will want to hear it, too. They're busy twisting Pussy Willow twigs together ready for waving on Palm Sunday."

"And we're going to decorate big floppy hats with them for Easter, too," Mary's young daughter told Gloria.

Gloria hadn't meant to mention her new idea to Mary until she'd told her how well everything had gone today. But she couldn't let such a good opportunity pass. "I was thinking about the prefab village's Easter Parade, Mary. It would be lovely if we could have a donkey leading it."

"You mean Moses?" Mary smiled. "It would be lovely, and I'm sure Moses would enjoy it. But how would we get him here, Gloria?"

"Bernard and I could fetch Moses and the cart here first thing Easter Sunday morning. Then everybody could set to decorating the cart and maybe the youngest kiddies could sit in the cart when we start the parade. They'd look so sweet if they all wear decorated Easter bonnets. Moses could wear one, too."

"John might be out of hospital by then," Mary said. "He wouldn't be able to take part of course, but seeing Moses would make his day."

"So, that's settled then," Gloria said, and then went on to tell Mary how her second day of tatting had gone. "Everyone missed John, though. Quite a few asked about him and said to tell him to get well soon."

"I can't begin to tell you how grateful I am, Gloria. Though I must admit I was a bit surprised when I realised your idea was for *you* to go tatting."

"Yes, it came as a surprise to Mum and Dad as well," Gloria said. "Dad's enjoyed himself this last two days, though, even though it's a lot different to driving her Ladyship round in that big car of hers."

"John thought it really funny thinking of your dad driving the cart," Mary said. "Nearly burst his stitches laughing, he did. I'm sure knowing things are going on almost as usual is making him recover quicker."

"Well, tell him he's not to get back to it too quickly, I'm more than happy to keep doing it. I reckon I'll be a bit sad when I'm not needed any more. Right now, though, I'll go home and give Bernard the news. Even though he isn't one for getting up early, he'll be chuffed to little pieces when I tell him he's coming with me on Easter Sunday morning to fetch Moses here to lead Broome Park Village's Easter Parade. And it's all because your John had his appendix out," she added.

"More like because you stepped in and went tatting," Mary said, laughing.

Travelling Tulips

"Mummy," said Jilly, peering out of the living room window, "I think Daddy's marked out a place for the sand pit. There's a sort of square shape in the lawn and it looks like some of the grass inside the shape has been lifted up a bit."

"I reckon that's wishful thinking, Jilly," said Doreen as she watched her two-year-old god-daughter, Elaine, dip toast soldiers into a softly-boiled egg - and creating a right mess in the process. "I asked Daddy last night when he'd get round to making the sand pit and he said he couldn't start anything until the weekend. It's a shame his firm don't have this week for *Wakes Week* like those round here."

"Someone's done something, Mummy. Maybe it was Paul."

"No. Your cousin only just got himself out of bed in time to do his paper round. He's got further to go from here than from his own house."

"Daddy might have got up early and—"

"Daddy won't have even *looked* at the garden. He's on an early shift at work so he left long before the Claytons' cockerel crowed to welcome dawn."

Doreen sighed. Bane of her life was that cockerel from next door but one. Woke Elaine every morning without fail. Still, Mary Clayton was generous enough with the eggs the hens laid, so she shouldn't complain. And, on and off, Jilly was best friends with the two Clayton children, so it would be hard to say anything really.

"Well, maybe some of Susan and Barry's hens came into our garden and pecked around then. Because there really are some lumpy bits of grass, Mummy. Oh, and I think the hens pecked at something in Mrs Stone's garden as well because she's out there with Miss Harper and they look a bit cross."

Doreen felt sorry for her two elderly neighbours sometimes; the other five prefabs on Broome Avenue had families with young children. It could get noisy when they were all playing out. Still, Connie Stone's three grandchildren who lived on Blakeley Road were often round at their Nana Connie's, so maybe the noise didn't bother Connie and her sister Flo.

But, thought Doreen, joining Jilly at the window after having checked Elaine was safely strapped into her highchair, something is definitely bothering them now. And Jilly's right. There are some lumpy bits of grass in our garden.

"You better go along to the Claytons', Jilly, and ask Susan and Barry to check if any of their hens are missing."

*

Jilly had been gone a few minutes and Doreen was outside the back door putting Elaine into her pram when Connie Stone arrived.

"Got something to tell you, queen," she said.

"'Morning, Connie. Come inside. Elaine won't settle if we're stood here chatting. Likely she'll start yelling anyway, bless her. I've only popped her in her pram until I get her playpen set up.

"Has something happened in your garden, too?" Doreen continued after Connie had followed her into the kitchen. "We wondered if the Claytons' hens had been pecking round in ours. Jilly's gone to ask Barry and Susan to check if any are missing."

Connie leant against the sink and sighed. "Flo and I were made-up when we moved from Liverpool and got a prefab here in the same village as our Pearl and the grand-kiddies. Shame we had to have hens next door and Broome Park at the end of the back garden, though. Because with them and all sorts of wild animals from the park, we do get a few plants dug up."

Doreen hid a smile as she visualised tigers and lions digging in their gardens.

"I mean rabbits and foxes, queen," said Connie, as if she'd read Doreen's mind. "But neither them nor next door's hens would dig up leeks and carrots and then put them back in the soil in a different place. And that's what's happened in our garden."

"I've not had chance to go and see yet," said Doreen. "But Jilly said it looked like someone had lifted up some clumps of grass in our lawn."

"Flo and me are entering our vegetables in the competition at the flower and vegetable show next month. It'll be the last time we do a joint entry what with Flo getting wed next week. Be her and Sam entering together next year. That's by the by, though. Today, we wondered if someone had dug up our leeks and carrots to see how big they were and then put them back in afterwards."

"Nobody would've dug up clumps of grass for that reason, though, Connie. Are you sure your carrots and leeks were put back in a different place? Maybe something pecked or dug around them and that loosened the soil?"

Connie shook her head. "We're very particular about the way we space out our veg in nice neat rows. They aren't in neat rows now."

Jilly came running back in before Doreen could say anything else to Connie.

"Guess what, Mummy? Oh, sorry. Hello, Mrs Stone. Mummy, guess what? All Susan and Barry's hens are there and there's no holes in the wire fencing around the hen run so they didn't get out and then go back in. But Auntie Mary…"

Jilly glanced at Connie. "She isn't really my auntie, Mrs Stone, I just call her auntie because Susan's my best friend. Anyway, Auntie Mary thinks some of the rocks in her rockery have been moved. And hens couldn't do that so it must be something else. Maybe a fox or a stray dog."

"We've ruled them out, Jilly," said Connie, going on to explain about her vegetables. "And don't you go thinking it might be them two grandsons of mine. Rob and Jimmy love playing tricks but neither of them would meddle with my vegetables."

"That's strange, Mrs Stone," said Jilly, frowning. "It's a bit of a mystery then. Like something in an Enid Blyton book. Or like the *Elves and the Shoemaker* and someone's helping out with jobs in our gardens instead of making shoes. Because where the grass has been loosened in our garden would be just the right place for Daddy to make the sand pit for Elaine to play in when she comes to stay. And maybe somebody thought your leeks were too close together or something."

"Well, slap me in the face with a finnon haddie. Do-good elves is one way of looking at it." Connie smiled at Doreen. "I'll get back to Flo now. I tell you what, though. Us two will be taking it in turns to watch out of the window tonight. If we catch an elf, we'll bring it round here for you, Jilly."

"What's a *finnon haddie,* Mummy?" asked Jilly when Connie had gone.

"Yellow haddock, I think."

Jilly giggled. "Mrs Stone says some funny things. I'd be in trouble if I slapped her with a bit of fish."

"You'd be surprised if she brought you an elf round," Doreen said.

They were still laughing when Paul got back from his paper round. Jilly told her cousin everything that had happened.

Doreen was surprised to notice how closely Paul concentrated. Aged eleven, almost six years older than Jilly, he usually thought he was too grown-up to listen to her tales.

"That's interesting, Jilly," he said. "Let's go and have a good look at the mysterious patch in your lawn."

Blow the washing-up for a few more minutes, thought Doreen and followed the two of them into the garden.

"It does look like a few clumps have been dug or pulled up and then put back in," she said. "I reckon Connie's right. This wasn't done by an animal. Maybe someone did want to check her carrots and leeks, but I can't think why anyone should dig up bits of our grass."

"Or move Auntie Mary's rocks around," added Jilly.

"I've got an idea," said Paul. "Maybe there was a robbery round here sometime and the robber thought he was being chased so he buried his haul in a garden. But it was dark so he couldn't see which garden. Or maybe it's quite a while since he buried it and when he came to get it he couldn't quite remember the exact spot."

"You've been listening to too many Sherlock Holmes stories on the wireless," Doreen told him.

"Or watching *Dixon of Dock Green* on his friend's television set," said Jilly.

"That's given me an idea." Paul grinned at them. "When I deliver his newspaper in the morning, I'll ask your very own Dixon of Dock Green - Policeman Ken of Broome Park Prefab Village - if there's been any burglaries round here."

"I think we would know if there had been, Paul." Doreen had tried to make light of his suggestion but, deep-down, she wondered if he could be right. That worried her. She didn't like the thought of a criminal wandering round the prefab gardens at night.

"Anyway," she added. "Standing here isn't doing any good. I'm going to set up the playpen for Elaine. Be a good girl, Jilly, and fetch some of her favourite toys."

"And I said I'd call for Anthony to go fishing," Paul said. "I wonder if anything happened in their garden. He was doing his paper round, too, so he might not have been out there yet."

Doreen glanced across at her other next door neighbours' garden. "Sheila's got her washing out. I'm sure she'd have noticed if there was anything different there."

*

Doreen stretched and yawned when the Claytons' cockerel, followed by the sound of Elaine bouncing in her cot brought her fully awake. She hoped today wouldn't be as hectic as yesterday had been.

Word about strange diggings in Broome Avenue's gardens had spread quickly and there'd been a constant flood of folk coming to have a look and give their ideas on what and why.

Apparently, there had been a burglary at Broome Hall a year or so ago - most of the families on Broome Avenue hadn't been living here then - but all the stolen items had been recovered. Nobody had heard of any local burglaries since then.

"It likely was a stray dog or a fox after all," she muttered as she jumped out of bed and hurried to take Elaine out of her cot before the little monkey bounced her way through the springs.

That explanation proved to be unlikely when, a couple of hours later, Sheila Grove came round from next door. "It's my tulips, Doreen," she said.

"What is? Put Fay in the playpen with Elaine," she added, smiling at her neighbour's pretty two-year-old. "I'll pour us a cuppa and you can tell me."

"They've been travelling," Sheila said. "Moved a couple of inches nearer the edge of my flowerbed. Someone must have dug them up and put them back in."

"Were you going to enter them in the competition at the flower show next month?" Doreen asked, remembering what Connie had said yesterday.

Sheila shook her head. "They won't still be in flower then. I only grow them because they look pretty and brighten the garden up."

"Well, it's got to be one of the older kids playing silly tricks. There's no other explanation."

"Whoever it was might have been wearing a cardie or dress that's got buttons like this. I found it in the soil where the tulips were before they got moved." Sheila reached in her pocket and pulled out a red, purple and green oblong-shaped button. "Unusual, isn't it? I don't remember seeing any like this, and I think I would have."

"Oh, it's so pretty," said Jilly, who'd wandered in just as Sheila produced the button. "Please can I have it for my button collection? I haven't got one that's anything like this."

"I reckon we should show it to Maisie Butterworth, her who lives on Knott Lane," said Doreen. "She makes frocks and other things to sell on her market stall and to folk round here. She might have sewn buttons like this onto something for someone."

"It isn't a market day today." Sheila stood up. "I'll pop round and get Fay's pram then you and I can go round to Maisie's, Doreen."

*

"Have you heard about what's happened in some of the gardens on Broome Avenue, Maisie?" Doreen asked.

Maisie nodded. "My girls told me about it when I got back from the market yesterday."

"Well, last night Sheila's tulips were messed with. And she found this." Doreen showed Maisie the button. "We think it might belong to whoever's been moving plants around."

Maisie nibbled her lip and looked worried as she gazed at the button.

"You know who it belongs to, don't you?" said Sheila.

"Yes. But she wouldn't go digging round in gardens in the night. I mean, why should she?"

"Why should anyone?" asked Doreen. "That's what we can't work out. But if you tell us who this belongs to, we might get an answer."

"I'm sure as eggs are eggs it wasn't her," said Maisie. "But she might be able to come up with an answer because she's got a knack for solving things. And *talk of Old Nick...*" Maisie looked up as Gloria Turner, her younger friend who lived next door and also helped her on the market appeared.

"Jeepers," said Gloria when the three others had explained things. "This is off the cardie I lent to a friend last week when she were going listening to that brass band playing in Broome Park.

"The bandstand isn't that far away from your gardens. Maybe the button fell off and one of those birds that like shiny things picked it up and then it dropped out of its beak when it was flying off somewhere with it."

"Sounds likely, I suppose," said Doreen. "We do get a lot of jackdaws and magpies." She sighed. "So we're still no nearer at solving the mystery of why someone should come digging things up."

"It solves the mystery of why my friend didn't return my cardie this morning on her way to work like she promised she would," Gloria said. "It's because she lost a button off it. She works lunch times at The Woodman on Thursday so I'm off to have a few words with her. I'll come back later, Maisie."

"And I promised Jilly she could ask Susan round for a picnic tea in the garden," said Doreen. They want gingerbread men biscuits so I best get back and start baking."

"I'll make some little fairy cakes if you like," Sheila told Doreen as they walked home. "Then I can bring Fay round and she and Elaine can have a picnic of their own in Elaine's playpen."

"The more the merrier," said Doreen, laughing.

*

Somehow, Doreen ended up with most of the neighbours in her garden. Even Connie and Flo had come round with one of Connie's grandsons. "We saw you were having a picnic, queen, so we made some lettuce and mustard and cress butties for the kiddies."

Naturally enough, talk amongst the grown-ups turned to the mystery of the strange happenings in their gardens. Connie and Flo had taken it turns to keep watch last night but neither of them had seen anything.

"And even though it must have took someone a while to move your tulips, we can't see your garden too well from our back bedroom window, Sheila," said Connie.

"Told you, Nana Connie," said her grandson, "it was aliens from outer space. If Captain Jet Morgan and Lemmy can reach the moon, them living on the moon can reach Earth and dig things up to experiment with them."

Doreen groaned. "Paul listens to *Journey into Space,* too. I'm going in to top up the tea pot and we'll all have another cuppa. I bet they don't get cups of tea in Space," she added.

When Doreen went back out with the teapot, she saw Gloria and a lass about the same age arriving in the garden from round the front.

"This is Natasha," Gloria said. "The friend who borrowed my cardie. And she's got something to tell you and the others who've had their gardens messed with. Looks like they're all here. That's handy."

Natasha took a deep breath. "It was me. I dug up things in your gardens but I put them back and I tried not to damage anything. I'm really, really sorry."

"But why, queen?" Connie was the first to recover from the surprise.

Natasha sniffed and wiped away a tear. "After we'd listened to the brass band playing in the park last week, me and my Raymond went for a bit of a... A walk round." She blushed as Gloria snorted.

"Anyroads, a bit later, we had a heck of an argument and it ended up with me taking off my engagement ring and chucking it at him. Only I'm a rotten shot and the ring went flying up in the air and I saw it land in one of the gardens. But Raymond stalked off and I went running after him to say sorry.

"He wouldn't make up so I thought *good riddance* to my ring and went home. I spent the next days in tears but I'd already decided to come and look for my ring when Raymond came round with a big bunch of flowers and a box of my favourite chocolates."

"And she came at night because she didn't want the world to know what had happened," said Gloria, taking over from her friend. "Only she couldn't quite work out which garden they'd been standing near. So she started from the far end and did three gardens and last night, wearing my cardie and losing a button off it, she searched the last garden along here."

"Never mind your cardie, Gloria. Did you find your ring last night, Natasha?" Doreen asked gently. She could see the poor lass was really upset.

Natasha shook her head. "It rained really heavy a couple of nights after my argument with Raymond. I think my ring soaked into the soil somewhere and it's lost for ever." She finished on a sob.

"I think we should all have a cup of tea and work out what we can do," said Doreen. "I'll send Jilly inside for two more cups."

She glanced round the garden but couldn't spot Jilly.

"I think she went round to ours with Susan a few minutes ago," said Mary Clayton.

"Sounds like they're back now," Doreen said as the sound of high-pitched voices reached them.

She frowned as she heard Jilly say, "She won't be cross. I'm sure she won't, Susan. I'll do it if you want."

"Do what, young lady?" Doreen asked as her daughter and Susan got close.

"Tell Natasha something," Jilly said. "Susan's scared to tell her," she added loudly.

Susan pushed Jilly to one side and walked up to Natasha. "Is this your ring?" she asked. "I found it in our garden, the one with the rockery and hens, last week. I didn't know it was special, honest, I didn't. I thought it was a toy one like you get in Christmas crackers. It's ever so tiny. I put it on my big walkie-talkie dolly's finger when I was playing going to a party with her."

"Natasha's got the teeniest fingers you ever saw," said Gloria. "Almost as thin as a darning needle."

"Oh, yes, it is my ring," Natasha said joyfully. "And it isn't a real diamond, nor real gold neither. But it *is* special. So, so special," she added, smiling as she took it from Susan and slipped on her third finger where it belonged.

"Well," said Connie. "This calls for more than a cup of tea. I'll nip round and fetch a bottle of the blackberry wine me and Flo made last autumn."

"And that sounds like the ice-cream van," said Natasha as a tinkly tune rang out. She reached into her handbag and pulled out a half-crown. "Go and buy a block of ice-cream to share with your friends, Susan. A treat for finding my ring."

The Wedding Day: Problems and Plans

"Mam, hasn't Auntie Flo told you anything at all about the dress she'll be wearing to get married in?" asked Pearl, glancing up from the book of wedding traditions and superstitions she'd borrowed from the mobile library. "You're her sister for heaven's sake, she must want to discuss it with you. Remember how me and Ruby were? We chose material together, made different paper patterns, went here, there and everywhere looking for buttons, ribbons, lace and such-like and—"

"It was different then what with you getting wed in war-time and our Ruby just after war ended," Connie said. "It weren't easy to get stuff so you needed to work together on your dresses."

"We'd have done that even if it hadn't been hard to find something right for our wedding dresses."

"Yes, but you were making them yourselves. Flo isn't. She's bought one. Why don't you read the tea leaves tell you what she's wearing?"

"It'd be Auntie Flo's tea leaves I need to read and she never seems to want a cuppa when she comes round. Likely she knows the tea leaves would tell me all about her wedding."

"I expect Auntie Flo thought she was going to be an old maid, Mum," said Babs, walking into the prefab's kitchen. "I think that makes her wedding extra special and she likely doesn't want anyone at all to see the dress before she walks down to aisle to marry her Sam. Me and Felicity are her bridesmaids and she hasn't even told us anything about it except when she took us to choose material for our dresses, she said the colours on the material we liked best would go perfect with her dress."

Pearl groaned. "And that material is pale green with flowers on. So Auntie Flo is likely to be wearing a green dress to get married in."

"Probably," Babs agreed. "It is her favourite colour."

"But it says in this book it's unlucky for a bride to wear green," said Pearl.

"We'll just have to have loads of things what bring good luck to cancel out any bad luck, Mum. There must be something about good luck in that book as well." Babs went over to look at it and turned a few pages. "See," she said, pointing, "it says it's lucky to give the bride *something old, something new, something borrowed, something blue and a silver sixpence in her shoe.* We can do most of that and you could make sure of the silver sixpence in her shoe, couldn't you, Nana Connie?"

"Yes, I reckon I could manage that somehow."

"What about this an' all?" Babs pointed to a picture of a chimney-sweep kissing a bride.

Connie nodded. "Seeing as Amos Whittaker is being Sam's best man, I'll ask him to make sure there'll be a *chimbley-sweep* standing by the lych-gate to shake Sam's hand and give my stubborn sister a kiss."

"At least getting wed on a Monday means she'll be healthy," Pearl said. "Shame it won't be a Wednesday, though. That's meant to be the best day of all to get married."

"Does it say anything about bridesmaids in the book?" Babs asked. "Only Maisie Butterworth showed us some patterns so Felicity and me could decide what style we wanted our dresses. There was a lovely one with a round neck, no sleeves and a sort of floaty skirt. Felicity said we couldn't have one with no sleeves 'cos that was unlucky for the bridesmaid."

"Can't see anything about bridesmaids, Babs," Pearl told her. "Shouldn't reckon it'd be unlucky, though, not in June when it's likely to be warm and sunny. Be different if it were winter, you'd get goose bumps on your arms in a sleeveless dress. But it's Auntie Flo's dress I'm worriting about. There mightn't be enough lucky things to cancel out the bad luck if she's wearing green."

Even though she didn't believe in superstitions and such-like, Connie didn't like to see her daughter so worried. "I'll go home now and have another go at trying to find out," she said, standing up. "I won't ask her outright, I'll chat about other things to do with the wedding and see if she gives anything away. But," she added, "if I find out she is going to be wearing a green dress, I don't know what you think we could do about it."

"We could appeal to Sam," Pearl said. "Get him to say he don't like the colour green or something. Auntie Flo wouldn't do anything to upset him."

*

All this flustering about Flo's dress is taking all the fun and pleasure out of things, Connie thought as she came out of Pearl's garden gate and closed it behind her with a little bang. *Maybe it'd be best to come straight out with it to Flo and tell her how bothered Pearl is. After all, Flo thinks the world of Pearl, always has done, right from the start. Bonded with her much more than she did with our Ruby even though Ruby was her first-born niece. And...*

Connie's musings were interrupted by Felicity running out of the Nobles' gate. "Auntie Connie," she said – she'd started calling Connie that as soon as she'd known her grandad Sam was marrying Flo, saying Flo would be her grandma so that made Connie her auntie-by marriage. "Auntie Connie, can I tell you about my big problem? Only it's to be a secret from Babs and the others. Mum says I'm being silly but I'm not."

Connie could see the young lass looked upset and wondered what on earth could be wrong. "Tell you what, Felicity, let's go for a little walk in Broome Park, likely we won't be disturbed there."

Felicity nodded and a few minutes later they turned into Broome Avenue and made their way to where it curved so they could go over the stile into the park. They stopped under an elder tree, admiring the clusters of white blossoms and Connie stayed silent, waiting for Felicity to talk.

"The blossoms are sort of silvery, aren't they?" Felicity said. "I expect my grandma-to-be would like some in her wedding bouquet if they're still blooming 'cos she says her wedding will be all silver and gold. That's because one of her and Grandad's special songs is *Silver Threads Among the Gold.* She said they've both got lots of silver threads in their hair."

"And they're having the hymn: *Daisies are our Silver, Buttercups our Gold,*" said Connie. "If Flo's calling it a silver gold wedding, I wonder if those are the colours she's chosen for her dress."

"'Might be. There's daisies and buttercups on the material for our bridesmaid's dresses and she said the colours go perfect with her dress. But, Auntie Connie, my big problem is *my* dress."

"Don't you like daisies and buttercups, Felicity?"

"Yes, they're really pretty. My problem is *this*," Felicity blurted out, pulling up the puffed sleeve of her blouse and pointing to a little mark near the top of her shoulder. "It's a birthmark, see, Auntie Connie, and it's so big and ugly I don't want anyone to see it and start laughing so I can't possibly have a bridesmaid's dress with no sleeves even though everyone says it'll be a warm day and a sleeveless dress would look right nice. And I know Babs really, really loves the picture of the sleeveless dress on the pattern Maisie showed us."

Connie really wouldn't have noticed the birthmark if Felicity hadn't pointed it out. But she knew it would be no good saying that to the lass. Even though it was many, many years since she'd been a young lass she could remember how sensitive and worried a blemish or not looking right could make you feel. Like the time she'd had a pimple on her wrist - above the glove line - and she'd...

"I might have an idea, Felicity," she said. "But I need to talk to your mum about it. Would that be all right?"

"Yes, 'cos she knows about this horrible thing, it isn't a secret from her."

"Trouble would be," Connie said, "if your mum will let me go ahead with my idea, I'd have to do it on Babs as well and she might want me to do it when the pair of you are together."

"So you mean she'd know about my birthmark then?"

"It might be best if you told her. She is your best friend and best friends shouldn't have secrets from each other, should they? Babs wouldn't laugh about it and she wouldn't tell anyone either."

"All right. But only if Mum lets you do whatever your idea is."

*

Two days later, Felicity and Babs chattered happily as they sat at a small table in Flo and Connie's prefab and watched Connie squeeze some yellow paint out of a little tube onto a tiny paintbrush. When Connie had finished with them, they were going round to Maisie Butterworth's to be measured for their bridesmaid's dresses.

Felicity's mum had been more than delighted when Connie told her she'd thought of a way to stop Felicity worrying about her birthmark showing if she wore a dress with no sleeves. Now, Connie was about to use paints to make the little mark look like part of a daisy.

"I'll do the centre part first," she said. "And I know the centre part of the real flowers isn't such a bright yellow as this paint but this will look good and when I've done the white petals and they've dried, I'll paint pink tips on them."

"Bright yellow's better for the middle bit 'cos it'll hide my birthmark more," Felicity said as Connie set to work.

"Your daisy will probably look nicer than mine 'cos Nana Connie can just paint over your birthmark but she'll have paint the centre of my daisy free-hand," said Babs.

"I'll have you know, I won prizes for my paintings of flowers when I was painting pictures more regular-like. And I'm thinking of starting doing it again once Flo's married. I can use her bedroom for a studio. Right, Felicity, that's the centre bit finished. Sit still while it dries and I'll do Babs' centre."

Half-an-hour later, Connie was about to paint pink tips onto Felicity's daisy when Flo came in. "Flo! I thought you'd be out for ages yet," said Connie.

"I found the right pair of shoes for my wedding day in the very first shop I went into," Flo told her, putting her shopping bag down on the floor. "But whatever are you doing, Connie?"

"I'm er..." Connie couldn't think what to say without giving Felicity's secret away.

"It's all right. I'll tell her," Felicity said. "She'll be my grandma in a couple of weeks so I don't think I mind her knowing."

"And I know what gave my big sister her idea," Flo said when Felicity had finished explaining about the birthmark and how Babs was having a daisy painted on, too, so they'd match each other. "It was something that happened around sixty years ago."

"Wasn't that many years back, Flo."

Flo laughed. "Near as makes no difference. She was eighteen or so, Felicity, and she were going to a dance with the lad who was courting her. On the day of the dance she got a whacking great pimple on her arm. And… and…" Flo broke off laughing again and Connie took over.

"I painted a bright red rose on my arm to try and disguise the pimple," she said. "So, yes, remembering that is what made me think of painting a daisy on you, Felicity."

"And," said Flo, going closer to look at Babs' arm, "my dress is all silver and gold so the colour of the daisies will match my dress, too. Oh, heck," she added, "I were trying to keep that a secret."

"We won't tell anyone if you don't tell why we've got daisies painted on," said Felicity. "It won't actually be these ones. Auntie Connie will be painting new ones on us on the morning of the wedding. These are for me and Babs going to be measured for our dresses so Maisie won't see my birthmark only a daisy."

"But listen, Auntie Flo," said Babs, "Mum's been that worried in case you were going to wear a green dress so can we tell her you aren't? And, Nana Connie, even though we know Auntie Flo won't be wearing green, can we still do all the good luck things we decided to do?"

"I hope you will," Flo said. "Not that me and Sam will need good luck but I do like all the old customs."

Connie hid a smile as she wondered what Flo would think of being kissed by a *chimbley-sweep*. She'd likely be happy about it seeing as she liked the old customs.

"Look," Flo continued, "I got this for Amos to sneak into Sam's jacket pocket." She opened her handbag and pulled out a tiny horseshoe. "And I bought some wrapped sweets as well," she said, "for me and Sam to throw at the kiddies when we come out of church."

"Oh, I can't wait for the day," said Felicity, "it'll be a lovely memory to take with us when we go to Australia. And, all right, I'll try not to get sad about that again 'cos me and Babs will still be best friends even when we're miles and miles apart."

"And when we write to each other, we can paint pictures of daisies on our letters so we never forget our last day together," Babs said, sniffing a bit.

Connie met Flo's eyes and smiled. She knew her sister and Sam were going to open a bank account for Babs and Felicity and put some money in as a present for their bridesmaids. Money the girls could add to so, when they were old enough, they'd be able to visit each other. Flo and Sam's wedding day certainly wouldn't be the last time they spent together.

Blackpool Blues

"What a bit of luck," said Jessie, glancing down Blakeley Road as she stood at the garden gate. "Rob Cole has just turned out of Broome Avenue. He'll be able to tell me if his gran's in. I know she tries to be around in case he calls in on his way home from work. She doesn't always manage it, though."

"It won't be so bad you walking round there and chancing bringing your rheumatics on if you know Connie's in."

The response was mumbled. Jessie sighed. Ted must have taken his teeth out again. He'd never get used to his new set if he didn't persevere. And the few minutes it took to get to Connie's was hardly likely to give her even a twinge of rheumatism.

Earlier on, Ted been worriting about the wooden yoyo he was making for Douglas Green next door asking her if it was really a suitable present for a ninth birthday. Then wondering if the yoyo might hit Douglas's spectacles - reminding Jessie of how the lad's mother kept a supply of Elastoplast especially for making temporary repairs on the nose bridge or the side pieces because her son was always damaging them.

"You know," Ted had said, "I won't be that popular if anything happens while Douglas is playing with his yoyo."

So, as much as Jessie loved her husband he was in a negative mood today both on his own behalf and hers as well and right now she felt like she needed a bit of a break from the daft h'aporth. She really hoped Rob would say his gran was home.

"Rob's almost here. You'd best put your teeth back in quickly, Ted," she hissed.

"Oh, heck." He sighed then turned his back to the gate and rootled in his pocket.

"Hello, Mrs Bailey. Hello, Ted."

"My, you look gloomy, lad," said Jessie after returning Rob's greeting.

Rob nodded. "Gloomy, fed up, down in the dumps. You name it and that's me."

"What me and Jessie would call *feeling bobbins*," said Ted turning round.

To give Ted his due, he didn't let on that he, too, had been feeling out of sorts all day.

"And why would that be?" Jessie asked Rob. "You didn't go and paint a door blue instead of green, did you?"

Rob was an apprentice painter and decorator. But, Jessie thought, he doesn't usually get too upset about mistakes. Maybe he's made a big one this time. The ones he'd told them about so far had been funny rather than serious.

"No, work's OK. It's the coach trip to Blackpool on Saturday. That's all Nana Connie went on about while I was there just now. She's so looking forward to it. She loves going to see the lights."

So that's answered my question, Jessie thought. Connie *is* in. "I think we're all looking forward to seeing the *'luminations*, Rob," she said. Though to be honest, because of the problem with his teeth, she wasn't that sure Ted was.

"She's including me in her plans," Rob continued, "and I didn't know how to tell her summat's happened and I don't want to go."

Jessie noticed Rob's furtive glance towards the prefab next door and wondered if a falling out with Sylvia Green was what had happened. She knew the two of them had being going round together.

"Want to talk about it, lad?" Ted asked Rob.

Rob shrugged and glanced quickly at Jessie.

Jessie hid a smile. Her Ted had become a sort of agony uncle – or seeing as he was nearer eighty than seventy perhaps that should be agony grandad – to the lads in the village. She guessed Rob would feel better talking to him on his own.

"I'll leave you two to it then. I'll be back in time for…" She'd been about to say *Blackpool Night* – Reginald Dixon was on it more often than not and both she and Ted enjoyed listening to the organist. Perhaps it was best not to mention Blackpool again though. "For our wireless programme," she said, nudging Ted away from the gate so she could open it.

*

"Here's my excuse for coming round, Connie." Jessie opened her handbag and took out the knitting pattern she'd promised to lend her friend.

"Jiminy Cricket, Jessie. You don't need an excuse. You're welcome any time. I'd of thought you knew that."

"I mean the excuse I gave Ted for coming round this evening when I'll be seeing you tomorrow at the *Knit and Natter* meeting. Told him you'd got the wool and if you had the pattern an' all you might want to start knitting your bolero for Blackpool tonight."

"Wouldn't most fellas have been chuffed at a bit of time to themselves?"

"Ted would usually but, bless him, he's got a bit of a cob on. Hopefully, trying to get to the bottom of what's made your Rob down in the dumps will make him forget his grumbles for a while."

"I thought there were something bothering Rob," said Connie. "Do you think it's something to do with the weather making the men folk act out of sorts, Jessie? It's really close and stormy again."

"It's not the weather with Ted. It's his new teeth. He's got them for the top and the bottom and he can't break them in. Says the top plate is the wrong size and won't stay put. But he's had it checked twice. I'm right worried he won't want to come to Blackpool if he thinks his teeth might click and slip in front of folk. He hinted as much earlier."

"There's something he can get to help," said Connie. "I saw it advertised in one of my magazines. I'll go and make us a cuppa and then I'll see if I can find it."

While she waited for Connie, Jessie wandered over to the sideboard to glance at the framed photographs across the top of it. She picked up one of Connie's youngest grandson to get a better look.

"I like this photo of your Jimmy," said Jessie, showing it Connie through the serving hatch.

Connie smiled as she looked at it. "'E's as made-up as Larry there," Connie said. "Not that I'm sure who Larry is," she added laughing.

Jessie was more interested in what Jimmy was holding than in who Larry might be.

"That's an *I-Spy* book he's got there. Does he like them? Only I bought two to give Douglas for his birthday. One was for things to spy at the seaside. I reckoned that'd be good for him to bring on the trip to see the 'luminations."

"Good idea, that is. We'll be getting there mid-afternoon so there'll be plenty of time for spying things before the lights come on."

"Ted didn't seem too sure Douglas would like the books with them not being storybooks. Mind, he didn't seem too sure about anything today."

"Jimmy thinks that getting an I-Spy book is the best thing to 'appen since sweets came off ration three year back," Connie said as she came back into the living room carrying a tray. "That's why he's looking so happy."

"So, seeing how he and Douglas are friends, Douglas will probably be chuffed to get a couple," said Jessie.

"That's one thing off your mind then, queen. Let's see if we can solve the problem of Ted's teeth while the tea brews."

*

When Jessie woke the next morning she turned over to gaze thoughtfully at Ted who was still asleep.

What excuse, she wondered, can I give him for going shopping? It wasn't her day for making the twenty minute bus journey to the nearest big shops. Especially when Reg's mobile grocery van was due in the prefab village today. But it wasn't likely Reg would have what she needed.

Jessie didn't want to tell Ted about the advertisement Connie had shown her last night for *Dr. Wernet's Powder* in case she couldn't get any. She was hoping to buy a tin so Ted could sprinkle a little of the powder on the plate of his false teeth to help them grip.

Ted was fidgeting now and Jessie guessed he was about to wake. Even after more than fifty years of marriage she still loved the moment he opened his eyes and looked towards her with a smile and a "'Morning, love".

This morning he added quickly to his usual greeting.

"I don't suppose you could make a little trip to *Woolies* to get me some of that special string I need for Douglas's yoyo? I can't go because I need to finish smoothing the wood so the lad won't get splinters. And, although young Rob said he'd try and go hisself first thing on Saturday morning, he also said that would only give him a few hours before the Blackpool trip to see if Sylvia would make things up. So happen you could see if they've got that record that he thought would be a nice way of letting Sylvia know how he feels."

Ted had told Jessie last night that he'd suggested Rob bought a little something for Sylvia to show her he was missing her and hoped they could make up. Apparently, Rob had said that was a corking idea and thought a recording of a song he and Sylvia liked might be the thing.

"*Sweet Heartaches*, it's called Jessie," Ted added. "Don't go anywhere else for it though if Woolies haven't got it. Their records are half the price of any others and Rob can't afford to pay out nearly ten bob."

Although she'd wanted good reason for going shopping, naughtily, Jessie pulled a face and pretended to think. Then she said, "I suppose I might be able to. If we get breakfast over and done with quickly, I'll get the ten o'clock bus."

*

"So," Jessie said to Connie on the morning of the Blackpool trip - she'd popped in to see her after buying some new laid eggs from her friend's neighbour, "Douglas was right chuffed with his I-Spy books *and* the yoyo Ted made him. Ted's really looking forward to the trip because, thanks to you and Doctor Wernet, his teeth feel safe and comfortable now when he's talking or eating."

"And thanks to whatever Ted said to Rob three days back, Rob and Sylvia have made up and they're definitely coming on the trip," said Connie, smiling as she spread *Echo* margarine on the bread she'd sliced.

"I'm right glad about that," she added. "I know Rob will want to spend most of his time with Sylvia but it'll be nice for me to have a while with them. Even though he's a working man now, I like to make all his favourite picnic food when we go on an outing. 'Mongst other things, I'm making cold sausage and tomato ketchup butties."

"Ted reckons a picnic isn't a picnic without Scotch eggs," said Jessie. "And new-laid eggs are best for making them so it's champion your neighbour keeping hens."

"Trouble with cooking sausages and Scotch eggs is the mess they can make of your frying pan if you're not careful," said Connie. "More often than not I end up having to clean mine with a *Brillo* pad and they hurt my hands something rotten."

"Haven't you seen those rubber gloves that are new out, Connie? *Marigold* they're called. I treated myself to a pair from the chemist's when I bought the Dr. Wernet's for Ted. They aren't that easy to put on and they feel a bit strange once they are on but they stop you getting sore hands."

"That's good to know. D'you reckon I could get the charabanc driver to stop at a chemist's on our way to Blackpool?" she said, laughing.

"Doubtful. And if I don't get a move on now, I won't be ready when the coach for Blackpool arrives and Ted will want to be one of the first to get on. He won't want to miss a second of anything he really loves an outing with friends."

*

Ted was feeling more than a little bit out of sorts as he sat on a bench in his garden shed. He'd decided he wouldn't be able to go on the trip after all.

He was pondering on how to break it to Jessie, when the shed door opened and Douglas from next door came in.

"Our Sylvia said she's just been round and you told her you're not going to Blackpool," he said. "I'm not going, neither, so can I stop in here with you, Mr Ted?"

"Why aren't you going, lad?" Ted asked. "I thought you were right excited about it."

Douglas sniffed and held out his spectacles in two parts. "They're broke and last time they got broke Mum said if happened again she wouldn't mend them. I can't see much without them so it won't be any good going to Blackpool, will it?

"Anyway," Douglas continued sitting down next to Ted on a wooden bench, "when Mum mends them she uses Elastoplast and they look a right mess. Everyone notices them more than ever and they start calling me *Specky-four-eyes*. So even if she didn't mean it about not mending them I'm not going and I'll stay in the shed with you."

"That you won't," Ted told him. "I'll mend your specs and they'll look as good as new. Then you can go and have a good time in Blackpool."

It didn't take Ted long to do a small, neat repair on the plastic nose bridge of the lad's spectacles.

"They should last long enough for going to Blackpool and coming home." He ruffled Douglas's hair before handing him the glasses.

"Thank you, Mr Ted. But why aren't you coming? You were excited about it, too. You said so at my birthday party yesterday."

"I hadn't lost my Dr. Wernet's then. But now I have and if I can't be sure of certain things staying put, I'll have to stay put instead."

Somebody calling Douglas's name put a stop to further explanations. Ted watched the lad hurry out of the shed and up the path towards the front gate.

*

Jessie was opening her garden gate when Sylvia hurried over.

"Why isn't Ted coming to Blackpool?" she asked. "Everyone will be right upset. We all love your Ted."

"Of course Ted's coming on the trip," said Jessie.

"He isn't," said Douglas, arriving at the gate. "It's because he's lost Doctor Wernet, whoever he is. And something to do with things not staying put."

Jessie felt her face turn hot. She'd borrowed Ted's fixing powder last night to sprinkle in her Marigolds so they'd go on easier and she'd forgotten to put it back in the bathroom cabinet.

"Don't worry," she told her young neighbours, "I'll sort it out. My Ted *will* be coming to Blackpool."

Sylvia and Douglas cheered loudly.

And now, Jessie thought a few minutes later as she hurried down to the shed with the Dr. Wernet's, thanks to good neighbourliness all round, I reckon it really is safe to say that *everyone* really is looking forward to the trip to Blackpool and seeing the 'luminations.

With Every Christmas Card…

"Mum." Rob looked up from eating his bowl of *Shreddies*, "Would it be all right if I ask Bernard Turner to come round to help me make my Spitfire model? He's already had measles, so Babs being infectious doesn't matter."

"Sorry Rob," his mum replied. "The smell of the glue and stuff might make her cough."

Rob sighed. He was sorry for his sister being so poorly. He'd had measles last year – he'd woken up on his fifteenth birthday covered in spots. He could still remember how fed up he'd felt having to lie in bed with the curtains closed and not being allowed to read. But this time it was an epidemic and he was fed up now an' all what with most of his friends being badly with measles right when he'd got a few days off work. That meant there wasn't much to do except make his model. Now he couldn't do that. Unless…

"Well, would it be all right if I took my model kit round to Bernard's then? We could work on it in his garden shed."

"I've got a better idea, Rob." His mum got up and went over to push the living room door shut. "I don't want Babs to hear," she said. "Mrs Latham said we could borrow her *Dansette* record player and a few records to cheer Babs up. Just 'til Saturday. The youth club need it then. Why don't you see if Bernard wants to go with you to fetch it?"

Mrs Latham was one of the ladies his mum cleaned for. She lived on The Avenue - a fifteen minute walk away. Rob had been to her house before and... "That would be good, Mum. I reckon this afternoon would be the best time to go. Mrs Latham might offer a slice of her special chocolate cake then."

"It'll have to be this morning, Rob. She goes to her W.I. meetings Thursday afternoons. Never misses. One of their main organisers, she is."

"Right. I'll go round for Bernard now. He'll owe me big time for taking him there when he sees what there is to see. But I think I'll tease him a bit first."

Rob dashed off down Blakeley Road to the Turners' prefab on Knott Lane. "I've got to go to an old lady's house to fetch a record player we're borrowing for our Babs. D'you want to come with me, Bernard?"

"Can't see that'd be much fun. Must be something better to do with our time when I've only got two days left of an unexpected week off school because of the measles epidemic."

"Like getting under my feet and asking for something to eat every five minutes, you mean?" said Mrs Turner. "Sick of the sight of you, I am."

Rob grinned at her. He knew Bernard's mum didn't really mean it. "He'd be much better off coming with me," he said. "'Specially to somewhere there's loads of model aeroplanes to look at," he added.

"What? In this old lady's house, you mean?" Bernard demanded.

"Her grandson builds them. He lives with her. He was a Spitfire pilot in the war."

Bernard grabbed his duffle coat from off the back of a chair. "Come on then," he said. "Let's go."

*

"I reckon Douglas, Mrs Latham's grandson, will be at work today," Rob said when he knocked on the front door of the large detached house. "But he might be here on Saturday when I bring the *Dansette* back. You could come with me then as well if you want to see him. Don't forget to wipe your feet when we go in and talk polite," he added quickly as they heard the door being opened.

"Good morning, Robert," Mrs Latham said. "Come for the record player and records, have you?"

"Good morning, Mrs Latham. This is my friend, Bernard. He's come to help me carry them home."

"And to have a look at Douglas's models no doubt."

"We would like to do that, please, if you've got time," Rob said.

"Come along inside then. Mr Spalding from next door will be bringing the records round in a few minutes. He borrowed them last week for some event or other. You can look at the models until he arrives and I'll get on with writing my Christmas cards. I'm only about half-way through. I've another three dozen or so to do yet."

She led them into a room she called the Snug and waved a hand towards a large showcase before sitting at a large desk.

"Cripes." Bernard gasped as he gazed at the models. "Much bigger than the ones we make. I wish we could build ours to this scale."

"Don't think we'd have room for more than one or two this size. They'd be harder to make as well. Just look at all the detail on them. Bet you're right glad you came now, Bernard," he added in a whisper.

"You bet I am."

They were so busy admiring the models they didn't realise Mrs Latham's neighbour had arrived until they heard him speak.

"I've brought the records, Mrs Latham. Heavens above. What are you doing with all those five pound notes? Not robbed a bank, have you!"

Rob turned to see what the man was talking about. He'd only been interested in looking at the models; he hadn't noticed what Mrs Latham was working on at her desk. Bernard obviously hadn't either, else he'd of mentioned something

"I made a lucky investment in some shares, Mr Spalding, so I decided to treat my family and friends. They'll have a white Christmas because I'm putting a five pound in with every Christmas card I write."

Clever that was, thought Rob. *Fivers are white.*

"I've got company this evening," Mrs Latham continued, "so I want to get the cards written before I go to my W.I. meeting this afternoon. Then first thing tomorrow, I'll take them to the post office and send them off by registered mail."

"Very sensible," said Mr Spalding. He glanced at Rob and Bernard. "Are you the ones who've come to fetch the records?"

"They are." Mrs Latham answered before either Rob or Bernard had time to. "The *Dansette* is ready and waiting for you on the hall table, Robert."

"Right." Rob walked over and took the records from Mr Spalding. "We'll go now. Thank you very much for letting us borrow them, Mrs Latham. We'll bring everything back on Saturday morning."

"And thank you for letting us look at the models," Bernard said. "They're really super."

"I must go now, too," Mr Spalding said. "I forgot to mention, Mrs Latham, I'm going to visit my brother in Llandudno today and I must hurry because I'm getting the one o'clock train. I'm staying overnight and I won't be home until late tomorrow afternoon."

"Enjoy your visit," Mrs Latham said. Then she looked at Rob. "And, Robert, I hope listening to records might keep your little sister happily occupied for a while."

*

Babs was asleep when Rob and Bernard got back so they had something to eat and waited for her to wake up. And at half-past one, they heard her calling.

She was thrilled when they took the records and record player into her.

"Bernard's staying for a while," Rob told her. "Mum checked with his mum and it's all right. We're going to look after you while Mum goes to do Mr Hargreaves's cleaning. She'll only be a couple of hours and one of us can go round and fetch Auntie Arlene if you feel poorly."

"There's a Max Bygraves record here," Bernard said. "*Gilly Gilly Ossenfeffer*. Shall we have that one first?"

"All right," Rob agreed. "But you hadn't better sing along too much, in case it makes you cough, Babs."

They'd played almost all the records when Rob checked the time. "Mum should be home soon, Babs," he said. "We'll just play one more record and then I'll go and put the kettle on. She likes a cup of tea the second she gets in."

Their mum walked in before the record had ended. Laughing, she joined in the chorus of *She'll be Comin' Round the Mountain*.

They were all "*eye-eye, yippee, yippee eye-ing*" when a tremendous rumbling from outside made the needle screech across the record as the prefab shuddered and shook.

Babs dived under the bedclothes but Rob and Bernard dashed outside.

"Cripes!" yelled Rob pointing at a huge aircraft silhouetted inside the low clouds. "What *is* it?"

"Land Sakes," yelled Arlene Whittaker running out of her prefab. World War Three hasn't started has it?"

"It's a Convair B-36," said her elderly dad who'd followed her out. "Reckon it's on its way to Burtonwood, there's still some of the United States Air Force based there."

"Is that the one they call Peacemaker?" Betty Jones asked as she and her husband, Tom, hurried up with a few more folk from the neighbouring prefabs. "'Tisn't very peaceful, is it?"

"It's super," shouted Bernard. "It must be circling to burn off fuel or something. Bit of luck it isn't properly dark yet else we'd hardly have been able to see it at all."

"You don't reckon it's going to make an emergency landing in Broome Park," do you?" asked Arlene, sounding nervous.

"Don't think so," Rob said after a while. "I think it's stopped circling. It seems to be moving away."

Everyone started to drift homewards when they could no longer see it. But they heard the noise from the six piston engines for some considerable time.

"I bet there'll be something about this in tomorrow's *Evening News*," Bernard said to Rob.

"Yes, we'll go and buy the early edition."

"Right. I'll come round in the morning and we can listen to records for a bit then we can go and get a paper about half-one," Bernard said. "I best get off home now."

*

"Can't you three play another record, Rob?" said his mum as she walked into Babs' bedroom with drinks for him, Babs and Bernard. "I think I'll go mad if I hear that *Laughing Policeman* song one more time."

"Bernard wasn't here the first twice we played it," Babs said. "So we put it on for him to listen to."

"Looks like Policeman Ken's come to have a listen an' all," said Bernard who was sitting by the window. "He's coming up the path."

Rob jumped up to turn the sound down as him mum hurried out of the room. She'd have his guts for garters if Policeman Ken was here to complain about the noise.

A couple of minutes later his mum called him and Bernard into the kitchen. "Policeman Ken wants a word with you," she said.

"Sorry about the noise," Rob said quickly.

"He isn't here about that, Rob." His mum shook her head. "Though it wouldn't have surprised me if he were."

"It's about yesterday, lads, when the two of you went to Mrs Latham's. Could you tell me about it? What you did, what you saw?"

"We saw the most super model aeroplanes," Bernard said.

"And what was Mrs Latham doing while you were looking at them?"

"She was sitting at her desk," Rob replied. "Said she wanted to finish writing her Christmas cards."

Policeman Ken nodded. "Did you see her writing them?"

"No, we were looking at the models."

"Her neighbour, Mr Spalding I think he were called, he saw her doing it," Bernard said. "Remember, Rob, he asked her if she'd robbed a bank because she had some five pound notes. She said she were putting one in with every Christmas card."

"Cripes, is that what's up?" demanded Rob. "Has she robbed a bank?"

"Of course she hasn't, Rob," his mum said. "Mrs Latham is a good, honest person."

"I'm afraid it appears to be Mrs Latham herself who has been robbed," Policeman Ken told them. "She said she left the cards on her desk when she went off to her W.I. meeting. She had intended to take them to the post office to send by registered mail this morning."

"Yes, I remember her saying that to Mr Spalding," said Rob.

"But when she returned from her meeting, the cards she had already addressed weren't on her desk," said the policeman. "Neither were the remaining five pound notes she'd left on it to put in with the cards she still had to write."

"You mean someone broke in and burgled her while she were out and took Christmas cards and money along with other stuff?"

"There was no sign of a break in." Policeman Ken frowned. "Apparently, Mrs Latham always leaves a spare door key on a ledge above the front door and, unfortunately, quite a few people know about it."

"Times I've told her she didn't ought to do that is nobody's business," said Rob's mum.

"If only she'd listened, Mrs Cole," said the policeman. "But now, lads, I want you to think carefully. When you left Mrs Latham's house, did you see anyone?"

"Only Mr Spalding," said Rob. "He left when we did. Said he were hurrying because he had a train to catch."

"Mrs Latham mentioned that," said Policeman Ken. "He isn't due home until later today. I'll have a word with him then and asked if he noticed anyone hanging around. I'll be off now, but if either of you remember anything else, let me know."

Rob and Bernard discussed it for ages after the policeman had left but they were both sure they hadn't seen anyone else in the avenue. But Rob did recall something Mrs Latham had said.

"When she let us in she said she was half-way through writing her cards and she'd another three dozen still to do. That makes seventy-two cards and if she were putting five pounds in every one of them..."

"Crikey. The thief went in to steal other stuff and went off with three hundred and sixty pounds an' all. He probably weren't expecting that."

"I hope they catch whoever did it," Rob said. "Shame we never saw anything suspicious."

"We saw something unusual yesterday, though, didn't we? Oh, not when we left Mrs Latham's but later on." Bernard moved one hand around in the air and made a growling noise.

"Right. The B-36. Let's go and see if the early edition of the *Evening News* is in yet."

Mrs Latham and her Christmas cards were forgotten for a while as everyone Rob and Bernard met on their way through the prefab village to the newsagent's on the main road talked about the huge aeroplane they'd watched the day before. When Rob said they were going for a newspaper to see if there was a write up, Betty Jones and a few of the others asked him to buy them a paper if there was something about the aeroplane in.

There was a good write up and a photo as well. Rob and Bernard spent the rest of the day listening to records with Babs and drawing pictures of the B-36.

"Don't forget we're taking the record player and records back in the morning," Rob said as Bernard was leaving to go home.

"Don't either of you dare mention the burglary," Rob's mum warned. "It might upset Mrs Latham."

*

Rob was really pleased when it was Douglas who answered the door when he and Bernard arrived at Mrs Latham's next morning.

"How's the modelling going, Rob?" he asked as they walked down the hallway.

"I've got a kit for a Spitfire, but haven't got round to starting it yet," Rob replied.

"It's a much smaller scale than your Spitfire," Bernard said. "Yours is terrific."

"Mr Spalding is here taking a photo of that and one or two others," Douglas said, leading them into the Snug.

Rob and Bernie put the *Dansette* and the records on a table and went over to the showcase.

"Hello again, lads," Mr Spalding said. "I was telling my brother about these models when I went to visit him on Thursday afternoon. He asked me to take some photos and send them to him."

"They'll need to be good photos to do them justice," Rob replied before looking at Douglas and asking if he'd built a model of the B-36.

"Ah, you saw the Peacemaker the other day did you?" Mr Spalding asked. "It was so low when it flew over my house the whole building trembled. I really thought the monster was about to lift the chimneys off the roof."

Rob nodded. "We'd better go now, Douglas," he said. "We've got to—"

"Rob," Bernard protested, "I wanted to ask Douglas about—"

Rob nudged his friend in the ribs. "Ask him next time. We've got to go."

"I'll see you out," Douglas said. Rob heaved a silent sigh of relief. He'd been counting on Douglas saying that.

When they reached the front door he said quietly to Douglas, "Mum said I wasn't to mention the burglary but… Listen. On Thursday morning, Mr Spalding told your mum he was catching the one o'clock train to Llandudno to go and see his brother. He just said in there about being with his brother Thursday afternoon. So how could he have seen that B-36? It was half-past three when it was circling the area."

"You seem very sure of the time, Rob."

"I'd checked a few minutes earlier. Mum was due home and I was going to put the kettle on ready for a cup of tea."

"That's right," Bernard agreed. "You said we'd time to play one more record first and your mum walked in just before it ended. And a couple of minutes later we heard the noise and dashed outside and saw the plane. When it moved away from the prefab village it would have passed over the houses here. We could hear it for quite a while."

"Rob," demanded Douglas. "Are you suggesting our neighbour had something to do with—?"

"He saw your mum with the money she was putting in with her Christmas cards. He made a joke and asked her if she'd robbed a bank."

"And a bit after that," Bernard said, thoughtfully, "Mr Spalding said how he'd forgotten to mention he was going to Llandudno to see his brother. I bet he hadn't mentioned it because when he saw all the money he made up a lie about how he wouldn't be here."

"So he could come in and get the money while your mum was at her meeting and nobody would think it was him who'd stolen it because they thought he weren't here," added Rob. "And after he had done it, he just hid inside his house 'til the next afternoon."

"Right," Douglas said, frowning. "You two get off home now and I'll telephone the police, tell them what you've told me and keep Mr Spalding talking until they arrive. I'm sure a constable will be round to see you later to get a statement from you."

*

"It all happened just the way you two worked it out," said Constable Boyce the following evening.

"Did Mr Spalding confess easily, Policeman Ken?" Rob asked.

"Or did you have to put pressure on him?" added Bernard.

"Once we pointed out how he'd given himself away by mentioning the B-36 flying low over his house, he admitted to the crime," said Policeman Ken. "He'll be dealt with accordingly."

"That B-36 will be remembered for more reasons than one," Rob said. "Dunno about Peacemaker, it should be called Crimesolver because if it hadn't flown over on that day at that time…"

"Mr Spalding couldn't have given himself away like he did," said Bernard grinning.

"And you know what?" said Rob. "We've got the measles epidemic to thank an' all. If I hadn't been given a couple of days off work and if your school hadn't been closed, Bernard, we wouldn't have gone to Mrs Latham's house on Thursday morning."

"What you might call a lucky break," Policeman Ken said, smiling.

"Cripes, it really was a lucky break just like Policeman Ken said," Rob commented to Bernard when they received an early Christmas present from Douglas and Mrs Latham: A model kit to build their own B-36 aeroplane.

Flo and Sam's First Christmas Together

Flo woke to the sound of Sam's gentle snores. Oh, how she loved to wake and know he was there beside her. Come Christmas Day, they'd have been married for six months. She still couldn't believe they'd found each other at their time of life. Not that they were really old, she told herself. Sam would be seventy-five soon and she were only seventy-three. But, until she'd met Sam, she'd thought she'd be an *old maid* for life. Sam had been married before though. Lost his wife in the war, he had, and lived on his own until he'd come to live in the prefab village with his son and family some sixteen months back.

Thinking of Sam's late wife, brought a little niggle to Flo's mind. *I bet she knew how to cook a flipping capon without it either drying up or bein' half-raw.* Poultry, which was only a twice yearly treat - Easter and Christmas - was about the only thing Flo couldn't cook. When she'd lived with her sister, Connie had always been the one to do that. Of course, if Connie had been here then she'd have likely come round to keep an eye on Flo's capon. But Connie had gone to visit her eldest daughter and son-in-law in America. Ruby and Walt had paid for her ticket and, after much argy-bargy-ing, Connie had agreed to go for Christmas.

Flo smiled to herself as she recalled what Ruby had written in the letter she'd sent her: *I'm sure you'll be able to persuade Mam to spend Christmas over here with me and Walt, Auntie Flo. I know you're a bit younger than her so she thinks she's the boss of you two but I fancy she'd listen to you this time. She'd never admit it but even though she'd still be going to our Pearl's for part of Christmas Day like you and she have done up 'til now, she'd be sure to feel a bit lonesome this year what with you and Sam being wed and no doubt wanting to spend all of Christmas alone together. I know Pearl agrees with this, we've been writing back and two about it for weeks and she'll help you talk Mam into agreeing.*

So it had all worked out well. Sam's son, daughter-in-law and grand-kiddies had gone to live in Australia just after she and Sam got married and, although she and Sam would go next-door-but one to see Pearl and Alf and the three kiddies on Boxing Day, they'd be celebrating their first Christmas Day and their six-month anniversary together, just the two of them. And the only fly in the ointment would be the capon she'd have to cook for their Christmas dinner. But that was three days away yet and maybe, now she was a married woman, she'd somehow be gifted the knack of cooking it to perfection.

*

In that dozy half-asleep, half-awake state of early morning, Sam reckoned he could hear his Flo's mind working at ten to the dozen. No doubt planning things out for the next few days. It were Saturday today, shortest day of the year, he realised, not that

Flo would be taking that into account. No, she was probably thinking of the Christmas cards they still had to write and deliver. They'd likely be doing that after breakfast.

Oh, they'd already sent those cards that had needed posting but these ones were for friends and neighbours in the village. He knew from last year it was a sort of unspoken agreement everybody delivered by hand and went into each other's prefabs for a mince pie or sausage roll – and, depending on what time it was, sometimes a glass of sherry or port or *Guinness*. Or maybe Flo was thinking of going collecting more holly from Broome Park. She'd said something about needing a couple of branches more for the living room. Looked perfect already to his mind and he'd enjoyed putting up the decorations and decorating the tree.

The little wooden figures and such he'd carved for Flo and Connie's tree last year looked a treat. They held a special place in his heart, too. Making them and taking them round to theirs one by one was when he'd first realised he had strong feelings for Flo. And now they'd be making memories of their first Christmas together. Actually, although they still did some things separate, like Flo going to her W.I. meetings and him going to The Woodman for a pint and a game of dominoes, they'd spent the last six months making memories of things they did together, hadn't they! And everything looked better and brighter somehow when they shared looking at whatever it was. Yes, every occasion, even walking round Radlington market on market days, had given them something to remember, like choosing and buying a capon yesterday.

He wished he'd had the guts to tell Flo he didn't like capon, chicken or any other poultry come to that. But she'd talked so much about how this would be their first Christmas dinner together, so excited, bless her, when he'd told her there'd be a nice stalk of Brussels sprouts what had been kissed by the frost ready to pick from the garden and he'd already dug up parsnips after the first frost and stored them in the shed in a box layered with sand so they'd be good for Christmas Day. If only there wasn't going to be that capon as well. Maybe he'd sighed because the next second he felt Flo wriggle and then she was looking down at him with a lovely smile on her pretty face.

*

An hour or so later, with breakfast eaten and cleared away, they sat writing out Christmas cards listening to *Uncle Mac* presenting *Children's Favourites* on the wireless. "Oh, listen Sam," Flo said, "he's going to play *Christmas Alphabet*. I love it when it gets to *M is for the mistletoe.* First time you kissed me was under mistletoe here at your Keith and Ellen's Christmas party."

"We don't need mistletoe to kiss under these days, do we?" Sam smiled and turned his face to Flo's to prove his words. "Strange to think, though," he said after their loving kiss, "how this time last year, I was a rather crabby fella living here with Keith, Ellen and my grand-kiddies and, now, it's you and me living here."

"You missing them, Sam?" Flo asked feeling a bit worried.

"Only sometimes and only a little bit, love. But us being together more than makes up for that. How about you? You must be missing your Connie a bit."

"Although it's lovely writing: *With love from Sam and Flo* on the cards, it feels right funny signing them from you and me instead of me and Connie. Afore she went off to Ruby and Walt's I did tell her I'd put her name on our cards as well seeing how she wouldn't be here to write and deliver any. But she gave me a little pile of cards she'd already written so we could hand them out with ours."

"And when are we planning on handing them out?"

"I think maybe do some this evening, before we settle down to watch *Saturday-Night Out* at seven-thirty." She saw Sam smile and nod before they both glanced across to their new television set. It was their Christmas present to themselves. Had a seventeen-inch screen, it did, so much nicer to watch than the one with a tiny screen that Keith and Ellen had left behind. "We can pop along to Pearl and Alf's first, Sam. See if my great-niece and great-nephews enjoyed themselves at the cinema last night."

"I'm sure they will have done, Flo. It was a right good idea of yours for their Christmas present from us to be money to go and see *White Christmas* and enough for ice-creams and stuff while they were there."

"And they'll still have the little bits of things from us for Pearl to put in their stockings," Flo said. "She seemed a bit down in the dumps when I saw her yesterday. Think she's still put out at Alf having to work late on Christmas Eve. I wouldn't of thought a warehouseman would have much to do in a soap factory then, would you?"

"Probably needs to make sure it's all clean and neat and tidy for when they go back after Christmas."

"Yes, that's likely it. Anyhow, like I were saying, I thought we could hand out some of these cards this evening, some after church tomorrow and any we don't get round to on Christmas Eve."

"Sounds good to me. What about this afternoon. Any plans for then?"

"You can sit and watch *Gardening Club* while I make some more mince pies. How's that sound?"

"Bliss. A right nice programme to see and a lovely smell wafting out of the kitchen while I'm watching it. Mind, everything you cook or bake smells good. Tastes good an' all."

Except probably for the capon, Flo thought. But, no, she must stay positive about that. It *would* turn out all right. Maybe she'd put it in the oven on a low light on Christmas Eve and give it a really long, really slow roasting. And for now, there was plenty more to think about and get on with. Only there did have to go and be a picture of a roast chicken on this card she was about to write, didn't there!

*

"I can't believe it's Christmas Eve already," Flo said to Sam as she watched him fiddling with the rabbit ear aerial thing on top of the television, hoping to get a good picture for *Stagecoach* starting in a few minutes. She wasn't over-keen on Westerns but she'd put up with this one because John Wayne starred in it. And with any luck they'd be tucking into roast chestnuts.

After they'd foraged in Broome Park for them a few weeks back, she'd sewn a bit of old net curtain into a sausage shape then Sam had put the chestnuts in and hung the *chestnut sausage* from a beam in his shed. He'd brought the chestnuts inside earlier and they'd put little slits in them before Sam had put them on a shovel, opened the fire doors and placed the shovel on the glowing coke. Flo sniffed. She was sure she could smell the chestnuts roasting already.

"Time does go quick when you're enjoying yourselves," Sam said now, sounding a bit breathless as he moved the aerial around. "There, Flo, love. "What d'you think of the picture?"

"It's all snowy," she told him with a giggle. "But I think it's meant to be. It's the weather forecast and a lot of places seem to have snow."

"Was trying here, earlier," he said, walking over to sit next to her on the settee. "Maybe our first Christmas Day together will be a white one. And we won't have to go out in it, if we don't want to."

"No," Flo agreed, a happy feeling spreading through her. "Nowhere to go or be except here. This room looks so cosy and Christmassy with all the decorations and the chestnuts roasting on the fire."

"Our own *Winter Wonderland* and we won't need to go in a meadow to build a snowman, we've got our own on the tree."

"And the cotton wool one I made to go on the table when we have our Christmas dinner," she said. Then wished she hadn't thought of that meal. She still wasn't sure whether to start the flipping capon roasting later tonight or leave it 'til morning. But the film was starting and she'd stop thinking about that problem for a while.

"I'm really enjoying the film," Flo said some time later. "But, even though I nearly burnt my fingers peeling them, I enjoyed the chestnuts more. I think I put too much salt on some, though, I'm parched now. Could do with a cuppa. How long to go before the end, Sam?"

"About ten minutes," he said. And just as he'd answered, there was a loud hammering on the front door and Flo heard Babs, her great-niece, shrieking.

"What on earth's wrong with her? And why come knocking at the front door instead of walking in the back door like usual?" asked Flo, jumping up and hurrying into the hallway.

"Auntie Flo. Auntie Flo. Come quick. Mum's proper poorly. Jimmy and Rob have gone carol singing with the church choir and Dad's not home from work. I'm frightened. She's got an awful pain."

Flo grabbed a coat from one of the hooks near the door, called for Sam to follow her to Pearl's and hurried off.

*

"Mum thinks it's her appendix," Babs said as they dashed past the Whittakers' prefab. "What if she has to go to hospital, Aunty Flo? It's Christmas Day tomorrow."

"Doesn't matter what day it, is, lass, if she has to go, she has to. And she'd be in the best place if it's appendicitis. But let's wait 'til I get inside and see her. If we need an ambulance, I'll send Sam to Policeman Ken's to phone."

Flo made her way into the prefab, flinging off her coat in the hall before going into the living room where she could hear her niece groaning.

Pearl was half-sitting, half-lying down on the settee clutching her tummy. "Babs, go and put the kettle on and make us a nice cup of tea while I have a proper look at your mum," Flo said, walking over to Pearl.

"Pearl, love," she said a few minutes later, "the last time I saw you like this was when you were givin' birth to Rob in the air-raid shelter back in May forty-one."

"I know when and where Rob was born, ta very much, Auntie Flo. But this isn't a baby. Good grief, I know I've put on a bit of weight recently but..." she broke off to groan again, "...I'm going through the change. Mam piled it on when she went through it and you never thought she were expecting. 'Sides, you might have been there when Rob were born but you not being married 'til a few months back and past it now anyway, that's likely all you know about anyone having babies."

"I know you were rude and stroppy that time an' all," Flo told her. "And we'll soon see if I'm right or not. Here's my Sam and I'm sending him to ask Policeman Ken to go and fetch the doctor. He might get here quicker than an ambulance."

Flo moved away to have a quick word with Sam. "She says she can't be having one but I'll eat my hat if she don't end up with a baby in the next hour or so."

*

It was a little longer than an hour but, at one minute past midnight, Pearl gave birth to a baby boy. "Six pounds, six ounces," the midwife said. The doctor had sent for her when Pearl had refused point-blank to go to hospital. "And he's a right beauty, this Christmas Day baby," she added, smiling round at Flo, before placing him across Pearl's tummy.

"He's a blinkin' miracle, that's what he is," Pearl said, all happy and good-tempered again. "I think we might call him Michael. That's the nearest I can get to miracle."

"I'll go and give the others the news," Flo said and bustled off into the kitchen where her Sam, Alf, Jimmy, Rob and Babs were sitting around the ironing board they'd pulled down to use as a table.

"I still can't understand how it happened," Alf said, shaking his head. "I mean me and Bead being parents again."

Flo swallowed a lump in her throat. She loved Alf's affectionate nickname for Pearl.

Rob was smirking. "You ought to have listened to yourself when you told me about the birds an' the bees, Dad. You'd of known then."

Alf gave him a gentle cuff around the head before jumping up. "I'm going to take a look at my new son," he said, "and I hope he grows up as good as you three kids, though maybe not as cheeky as our Rob," he added over his shoulder as he went from the room.

"I think we might like having a baby brother," Babs said.

"I will, Jimmy told her. "It means I'm not the baby of the family now."

"I bet the lads at work will get at me something rotten having a baby brother almost sixteen years younger than me," Rob said. "I mean, Mum and Dad are getting' on a bit for… for being parents again," he finished after Flo had given him a gentle kick.

"Never mind all that. When can we see him?" Babs asked. "And what are we going to do about our Christmas dinner? I always help Mum make it but I can't do the lot on my own."

"The midwife will call you in as soon as she's tidied up," Flo said. "She knew your mum didn't realise about baby Michael coming so she brought some baby clothes and nappies with her. He'll have to sleep in a drawer 'til we can get a carry-cot from somewhere."

"He can sleep in my dolls' pram," Babs said, "it's a nice big one, remember, Auntie Flo. Some of my dollies' clothes might fit him an' all 'til we get him some of his own. But what about our Christmas dinner," she asked again.

Flo glanced at Sam who nodded vigorously, "You'll all have to come round to me and Sam," she said. "And you can help me cook it, Babs."

"Have you got a chicken, Auntie Flo? Should I bring ours round? Can I be in charge of it? I'm right good at making roast chicken, you ask Mum."

"We've got a capon, that's the same as chicken really. I think it'll be big enough for all of us, and we'll keep yours for Boxing Day. And yes, I'll let you be in charge of cooking the capon if you like, Babs."

"I'm hungry now," Jimmy said. "Instead of leaving mince pies out for Father Christmas who we know is really Dad but we pretend not to, can we have mince pies to eat now?"

"I don't see why not," Flo said. "I'll make us all some cocoa as well. But after that, as soon as you've peeped into see your mum and your new brother, I think you'd all better go to bed. And you might not believe any more, but my guess is, when you wake up, you'll still find Father Christmas has filled your stockings for you."

*

It was another hour before Flo and Sam made their weary way home. "Not what we planned, Flo," Sam said, but it will be nice having them all at ours. And if there isn't enough capon to go round, I won't mind not having any. To be honest, love, I'm not that keen on capon or any other poultry to be honest."

"Oh, Sam. Why didn't you say? Not that it matters now because Babs will see to it, but I've been dreading trying to cook the dratted thing and to think we could've settled for a nice joint of beef or pork. I can cook them all right."

Laughing, Sam opened their front door and they went inside. "That'll teach us to keep secrets from each other."

Flo nodded. But she did have one more secret and that was the watch she'd bought for him, even though they'd said they weren't buying each other anything because the television was their present.

"I bet Connie will be surprised when she comes home and finds out she's got another grand-child to call her Nana Connie," Flo said a short while later as they snuggled down under the bed clothes. "And we're a great-auntie and great-uncle again."

"So we are," Sam agreed, chuckling. "Oh, and I know it's only very early Christmas morning but..." He reached under his pillow and pulled out a small, prettily-wrapped package. "Happy Christmas, Flo."

Flo reached under her pillow and pulled out her present to Sam. "Happy Christmas, Sam. Let's open them together."

"We'll never forget our first Christmas together, will we, love?" Sam said as, a few minutes and a few kisses later, they finally settled down to sleep - both wearing the watches they'd secretly bought for each other.

Acknowledgements

Some of these prefab village stories made their first outing on the pages of The People's Friend magazines. A special thank you to David Young who illustrated those stories and brought the characters alive for me and everyone who read about them. He just had to be my choice for the cover artwork!

Massive thanks to Jo Bartlett and all at Fabrian Books for their help and advice.

To everyone who asked for more Broome Park Prefab Village stories: I hope you enjoy this Collection.

To everyone who lived in a prefab in the 1940s and 1950s - or knew someone who did - I hope these stories bring back happy memories.

Also available from Pat Posner this Christmas

Fake Fiancé for Christmas

(A Fabrian Books' Feel-Good Novel)

Best friends Flora and Val, will usually do anything for each other.

But Flora refuses to pretend she's engaged to Val's brother when Val says it will scotch the rumours about Bryce so their uncle won't disinherit him.

True, many years ago, as a very young teen, Flora idolised Bryce. She's learned the hard way to stop doing that, though, and it's no surprise to her when Bryce ridicules his sister's idea. But then...

Flora and Bryce discover Val has a desperate reason of her own for needing their pretend engagement. So, for Val's sake, even though acting as if they even like each other will be hard, they agree to go along with the idea.

They'll tell their families they want to keep their engagement a secret until after Val's Christmas wedding so as not to take the limelight away from her.

Because it will only be family who'll think Flora and Bryce are engaged, breaking it off after Val's wedding won't cause any more unwanted publicity for Bryce.

But Christmas is a few weeks away and playing a part to deceive others can sometimes misfire.

Available on Amazon.co.uk and worldwide.

Other books available from Pat Posner

Daffodil Days - Stories from Broome Park Prefab Village

And the Jukebox Played their Song - A Broome Park Prefab Village Novel

Christmas Wishes…New Year Kisses - An Oaktree Farmhouse Novel

Shadowed Love - A Little Village in the Dales book

Also available from Fabrian Books

Christmas in Switzerland

By Melinda Huber

Christmas is approaching, the Lakeside Hotel is full of English-speaking guests, and Stacy and Rico can't wait to show them a real Swiss Christmas. There's a visit from the Samiclaus, a Guetzli-baking demonstration, a snowman competition - not to mention the trip to Davos.

But in the middle of all the festivities, a guest has a huge problem and Stacy is left running backwards and forwards, wondering if she'll last the distance. And Rico's father is behaving very oddly, too.

It doesn't feel a lot like Christmas at Lakeside any more... Can Stacy get the magic back, before it's too late for her and Rico?

Available from amazon.co.uk and worldwide.

Printed in Poland
by Amazon Fulfillment
Poland Sp. z o.o., Wrocław

59926371R00115